THE ICERA STONE

*a modern day story with a link from the
pagan past*

Andrew Homer

To Adrian & Sue
Andrew

Bloomington, IN  Milton Keynes, UK

authorHOUSE®

AuthorHouse™
1663 Liberty Drive, Suite 200
Bloomington, IN 47403
www.authorhouse.com
Phone: 1-800-839-8640

AuthorHouse™ UK Ltd.
500 Avebury Boulevard
Central Milton Keynes, MK9 2BE
www.authorhouse.co.uk
Phone: 08001974150

This book is a work of fiction. People, places, events, and situations are the product of the author's imagination. Any resemblance to actual persons, living or dead, or historical events, is purely coincidental.

First published by AuthorHouse 6/28/2007

ISBN: 978-1-4259-6001-8 (sc)

Printed in the United States of America
Bloomington, Indiana

This book is printed on acid-free paper.

To Ellie

Contents

THE ICERA STONE
- THE PROLOGUE 1000BC –

The Firestar

ICERA AWOKE RESTLESS AND wide-eyed. Shadows haunted the hillside and the sun had yet to colour the sky. The afterglow of the twin fires warmed her face as she lay under the animal furs in her newly woven gown.

Throughout the dark days, the Hendas had been confined to their roundhouses. Now, for two nights, to herald the return of the sun, the tribe would sleep in bracken filled hollows with nothing but the stars and the moon above. Last night they had gathered upon the Hill, to crown her - Icera, their new priestess.

Icera stared at the shadow of the horned headdress as it danced across the Cernstone. It echoed the Shaman's movements of the night before when he had brought to life the spirit of the Osser. She watched the silhouettes of the carved beasts on the back of the oak throne move in unison with the firelight. Upon the seat, next to the silver torc, lay her crown. Icera rose and once more, she adorned herself with the floral circlet.

From under the goat-wool pillow, she retrieved her pouch and undid the drawstring to remove her most prized possession - her mother's brooch. She gazed at the twin bronze coils. At the centre of each, the two bowls of polished metal were as two souls touching. As they glinted in the firelight, in one bowl, she saw her own reflection. In the other, the face that smiled back had appeared to her many times before, except this night it seemed even clearer - it was her mother, Maia.

When Icera was three summers old, Maia had left this realm to cross the portal to the Otherworld and, since that day, her mother's spirit had watched over her as her star-guardian. Last night, at the ceremony, when she had turned seventeen, the right to follow on from her dead mother had passed to Icera.

After her mother's death, the tribe had chosen Icera to receive the secret of starcraft. She had journeyed to far-off clans and learnt about the cycles of the sun and the moon, and the special times when dark equalled light. She had studied well, until her consciousness was in tune with the movement of the heavens.

She skipped over sleeping bodies until she reached the edge of the precipice where the whole of the sky lay before her. The air felt charged as if Cern himself might strike his anvil and send sparks from the heavens. Hundreds of feet below, in the darkness of the wooded valley, the wind whined and whistled. A cold breeze funnelled up the cliff face and tossed her golden tresses from her forehead. Away from the fires, the air had a chill. She draped the dark red woollen cloak around her shoulders and fastened the brooch.

As she had done on countless cloudless nights, Icera fixed her eyes upon the cluster of seven stars that now, by their dawning, heralded the rebirth of the year. They belonged to her, they were her family and, of their number, Maia glowed the brightest.

Her heart missed a beat.

To others it would have been no more than a pinprick, as insignificant as a flake in a snowstorm, but to Icera, it was unmistakeable. She tallied up the dots of light. How could it be? There had always been seven stars, but now she counted eight.

The new arrival shone a shade more yellow than the other seven. As she studied the pattern, it changed.

Entranced, not daring to let the pale dot out of her sight lest it disappear and fade to dust, she watched the new star slowly move away to embark upon a journey across the wide formation of the Aurochs.

Soon the scratch of gold had traced a path from one edge of the constellation to the other.

As the star drew nearer, so did a distant memory of a tale told to her by her mother - a wondrous star of fire would proclaim the crowning of a priestess, who would then become a great leader.

Icera began to tremble. A sensation from the depths of her being rose through her. She arched her back and flung open her arms in an embrace to welcome the newborn star. She turned to the sleeping tribe and found an authority in her voice. The wind carried her words over the hollows. 'Hendas, wake up… the firestar comes.'

Bodies stirred and, with sighs and grunts, startled faces emerged from under the animal skins. A mounting sense of urgency took hold as, one by one, the tribe gazed at the yellow light. The longer they stared, the more its ultimate destination became inevitable. The night filled with shrieks and cries.

Shaman Woran grasped the silver torc from the throne and raced over to Icera to place it around her neck.

With the weight of the metal against her skin, she felt a protective force surround her.

Woran leant towards Icera, and brushed her cheek as he whispered her name. A piercing howl cut short his words. The incoming blaze burnt an arch across the red-tinged sky; over the tops of the trees, trailed a wake of fire.

Terrified tribe-folk dived under their furs. Frantic mothers grabbed their children. Some hid in hollows within the earth and took whatever they could find to protect them. Some cowered behind the Cernstone. Some huddled under the massive oaks. Hogs squealed in the pens and, in the woods, wild wolves howled.

The fur of their bedclothes caught alight. Woran threw his deerskin over Icera. The ball of fire screeched over their heads. It shot across the precipice, and down the cliff face into the valley.

Before the force of the explosion hit, a moment of silence punctuated the night. A searing white heat turned the darkness into the brightest day. The earth shuddered to a thousand drums and below, lay an inferno.

A whipcrack shot across the edge of the cliff. The ground shattered. A gaping split tore Woran and Icera apart.

'Icera, jump!' Woran threw open his arms.

The cliff edge gave way. Icera leapt. Woran caught her and they ran. Together they turned to see the face of the cliff collapse and fall into the firestorm below them. From a cloud of smoke, white-hot sparks shot like beads from a cauldron of molten bronze. The fire-draught tunnelled up the cliff wall and it glowed as yellow as a kiln. The force of the blast shot high up into the sky. Heat scorched their hair, and fused their eyelashes. They dropped to the earth and rolled over in the dust.

Paralysed by fear, the tribe-folk had gone to ground. Slowly, they now emerged. They gasped, coughed and spluttered in the acrid smoke, trying to rid their nostrils of hot ash.

Icera stood next to Woran, at the newly formed cliff edge. They peered down into the turmoil and shielded their faces, the light of the blazing forest in their eyes. The landfall had quenched the heart of the fire. They stared. Below them through the smoke, they could make out two glowing lights.

In the shadows, the voice of Awen, the old Crone cried, 'It has come… the gift from the gods!'

CHAPTER 1

The Anticipation

'OSSER?' ERICA LOOKED QUIZZICALLY across the breakfast table at her husband. 'That's a strange word.'

Simon was dismissive. 'It's a load of pagan hocus-pocus… some horny old monster. It's just the locals' excuse for a knees up.'

They had come to live in the Dorset hamlet of Upper Melbury three months ago, when Simon had been elected Member of Parliament for Wessex South. On most weekdays, whenever the House was in session, he stayed in their old apartment in Streatham. Sunday morning was now one of the rare occasions when they had a chance to talk.

'I suppose it might offer the chance of a photo opportunity,' Simon muttered into his newspaper. 'It's midday next Saturday.'

Erica spread jam on her croissant. 'That's May Eve, the day before our birthdays.'

'I might get you two a joint present this year,' Simon announced.

'That's what you always do, dad.' Sarah rolled her eyes. Their daughter was raiding the fridge, having breakfast on the hoof.

'So what's it all about, this village festival?' Erica asked.

'To mark the start of Spring or something,' came the crusty reply from behind the newspaper barricade. Simon paused to sip coffee. 'I understand they dress up and prance about outside the Green Man and then they parade up the Hill.'

'It all sounds very ancient and mysterious.' Erica was intrigued. She turned to her daughter. 'Sarah, if you're going to Liz's for a party for your seventeenth, you'll miss all the excitement.'

'Don't worry mum,' Sarah grabbed a banana and a pot of yoghurt as she headed for the back door, 'I won't miss a thing.'

****

'Mrs Janus, you'll kindly not use that word in my shop!'

On Monday morning, when her husband had returned to London and Sarah had left for college, Erica had driven into Witchbury to begin a quest - to seek out what might be discovered about the Osser. To utter the word aloud in the greengrocer's had been her first mistake. Miss Bird had reacted as though Erica had let out some heinous blasphemy.

The shopkeeper screwed up her thin lips and continued, 'You'll take my advice if you know what's good for you, stay away from the Skimmity.'

The rebuke stunned Erica. Her dignity dented, she made her apologies and hastily departed. She felt bruised - what had that scarecrow of a shopkeeper meant by advising her to keep away from the ceremony? How dare she…

Erica passed the window and caught sight of Miss Bird's face through the vegetable display. An image came into her mind - with that narrow face and wisps of grey straggly hair that stuck out from under the knotted, dirt-smeared, green rag of a headscarf, the grocer was the perfect likeness of one of her prized parsnips.

At nine the following day, Erica visited the village library to continue her mission. Bunty Bagwash, known as Beebee to the whole village, stood behind the counter sorting books. The tubby librarian wore a black skirt, yellow jumper and a necklace of large black baubles. Other than the librarian, there was one other in the library. Erica noticed him only when he poked his head around the end of one of the shelves. He was a diminutive man with a large nose and seemed to break off from studying a medical book, to spy upon Erica as she approached the counter.

Erica meant to be more guarded but the Osser word emerged from her lips louder than she had intended.

Agitated, Beebee tutted, 'Never use afore its time.'

Erica was bemused. Yet again, she felt like an admonished schoolchild.

Beebee gave a nervous glance toward the shelves, shuffled toward Erica and hissed, 'Beltane…' as if that were reason alone and an end to the matter.

Erica looked at her with a puzzled frown.

'It's like this, Mrs Janus; it's just not done…' she whispered, 'local tradition allows mention for only one hour after midday, on May Eve, otherwise…'

'A sort of bad omen, you mean?'

Beebee nodded, put her head down, and continued to rubber stamp a pile of books.

Erica shrugged and headed to the Mythology and Folklore shelf. She was still conscious of the little man taking an interest in her presence. After ten minutes, she gave up her search for any reference to the Osser and took a book back to the counter on a different topic.

The librarian's face softened slightly at seeing Erica's choice. 'Psychic Pets, how fascinating.'

Erica felt a little more cheered by her tone. 'Sometimes I think my dog Jet has a sixth sense.'

Beebee rested her bosom on the counter and leant across, as though about to impart some secret. 'There's always the County Museum in Dorchester, but the building is closed for refurbishment. I must warn you, if you're thinking of taking photographs,' Beebee looked stern, 'that's not welcome either.'

'Why ever not?' Erica enquired.

Beebee looked down to where the small man had been standing. 'Images of the Horned One are not allowed,' she replied, sharply. 'That's the rule, it's a bad omen.'

Erica was unable to avoid a touch of irony in her voice as she turned to go, 'Thanks for your help...'

As she left, Erica looked around for any sign of the man. No one else could be seen although she still had the feeling that she was being watched.

Simon had to attend late night sittings all week, culminating in a vote on anti-terrorism. It was Thursday evening before Erica managed to make contact with him. She sat down at the phone in the study and attempted to relate in as measured terms as she could about her encounter with the officious librarian, and the warning not to take photos.

For Simon, it acted like a red rag to a bull. 'Total nonsense, no photographs - whoever heard of a subject being out of bounds for a library - other than salacious sex, but most modern novels are full of that anyway. Bad omen, what does that mean? Ridiculous superstitious claptrap - for God's sake this is the twenty-first century.' He put the phone down on her in a temper.

Erica picked up the handset from the study and wandered into the kitchen. She was about to stir her hot chocolate, when as she had anticipated, the phone rang.

'I've been thinking...' her husband continued. 'It might work in my favour - all the better to give the story a sharper angle, even spice it up a bit? A touch of controversy is a bloody good idea; it'll give my image a bit of boost. As a new brooms around here, it might do me good to be seen to be sweeping away some of this old-fashioned thinking, we want to encourage tourism not keep things secret. If we can get the right pitch, it could even make the front page of the local rag. I'll give the editor a ring.'

Typical Simon, why had she bothered? Appeals for discretion always had the effect of goading him on all the more. To Erica however, the tradition of secrecy and Beebee's warning served to heighten the sense of mystery. Erica was more than willing to go along with the wishes of the local custom. After all, there was probably a good reason for the superstition, even if the justification had long been forgotten.

The approaching Saturday began to intrude upon her sleep. The forbidden word revolved around in her head... Osser... Osser... Osser.

By Friday afternoon, she was in a whirl and tried to decide what she would wear at the ceremony. As soon as Sarah returned from college, Erica was keen to talk through her ideas for an outfit. 'It starts at twelve tomorrow. I'll raid the boxes in the attic. We've not fully unpacked yet from moving, and things will have to be pressed.'

'I'm sure you'll look great, whatever you wear, mum.' Sarah gave her a smile. 'It's your big four-O, on Sunday,' she teased, 'I'll be back for that.'

'No chance of me forgetting the first of May as it's your birthday too.' Erica smiled. She suddenly noticed the clock. 'I must dash or I'll be late for your dad.'

When she collected Simon from the station in Dorchester, what his wife was to wear was the last thing on his mind. 'I don't care - just look the part,' he stated, grumpily.

Erica knew very well what he meant. He expected her to dress like the wife of a Member of Parliament.

By mutual agreement, even before moving to Corner Cottage, Simon and Erica had their own rooms. The prospect of being bedfellows no longer held attraction for either of them, although Simon, rather to her annoyance, still regarded her bedroom as an extension of his own territory. Their relationship had now become a partnership of convenience but a state that they both tacitly acknowledged might not be sustainable.

Erica arose from her bed on a bright Saturday morning. What had started as mild curiosity, barely a week before, had gathered such momentum she could now think of little else. Her husband sat at the breakfast table and her daughter was in the kitchen. Erica rushed over to the window. 'I must let the air in,' she exclaimed.

'What's up mum?' Sarah asked, 'You seem to be a bit stressy...'

Erica tried to play down how she was feeling. 'I just didn't have a very good night.'

Simon briefly looked up from his paper. 'Your mother's become wrapped up with all this Beltane hocus-pocus nonsense.' His gaze returned to his newspaper. 'We're not a bunch of bloody pagans you know.'

'Perhaps it would be better if we *were...*' Erica glanced across at the headlines announcing another suicide bomb.

He grunted.

What was it Simon had said in the car - 'Just look the part...' Well we'll see, she thought. 'I'm off to get ready,' she announced and threw a grimace at her husband.

Half an hour later, she returned wearing a white cotton seersucker dress with a broderie anglaise bodice. A red stole complemented the outfit, while on her feet she wore a pair of Indian mules, embellished with tiny circular mirrors. On a black ribbon, she wore her favourite necklace, an ammonite in a silver clasp.

Simon, was still at the table. He glanced up from the paper and raised his eyebrows. 'My god, Erica, you look like the bloody Queen of the May!'

'Well, it is May Eve,' she countered in frustration, 'I'm wearing red, white and black, the colours of a maiden, a mater, and a matriarch.'

Simon roared like a bull elephant. 'Don't you mean virgin, whore and old crone?'

'You just don't appreciate anything, Simon.'

Her daughter chipped in. 'You look great mum...' Sarah delved into her bag and found a drawstring pouch. 'Why don't you wear this, to finish your outfit off?' She took out a bronze brooch and pinned it through her mother's scarf.

Erica looked astonished. 'Sarah, how beautiful, wherever did you get that?'

Sarah sounded dismissive. 'Someone gave it to me.'

Erica felt uncertain. 'If it was a present to you, I don't think I should...'

Sarah interjected. 'You can borrow it. Be careful though, the pin's a bit wonky.'

'It looks ancient, are you sure? I love the way the spirals interlock. The artwork's so intricate.' Erica was spellbound. 'I can see your reflection in one bowl and myself in the other.'

Sarah stood up and grabbed her bag. 'Don't worry about giving me a lift into Dorchester mum, I'll make my own way.'

'Are you off already, dear?' Erica looked concerned. 'Thanks for lending me the brooch. It's wonderful.'

Her daughter headed for the door. 'Must dash, or I'll miss the bus.'

Erica called after her through the open window, 'I'll pick you up at five tomorrow, once I've dropped dad off at the station. Have fun at Liz's.'

Sarah ran off in the direction of the bus stop.

An hour later, Erica was staring out of the passenger seat of the BMW, on the way to Witchbury. Simon drove past Hobbs Cross, where the road turned off to the church. A sudden compulsion hit her. 'Stop, wait a minute!'

'Bloody hell, Erica, we'll not be in time to get parked...' Simon huffed and pulled up at the entrance to a field.

'Mayflowers... I need them for my hair.'

'My god, Erica, now you're letting this thing completely go to your head.'

Erica did her best to laugh off his remark. 'I'm just doing my best to enter into the spirit of the occasion.' She strode off toward the hedgerow. Along with mayflowers, Erica gathered daisies and buttercups. When they were underway again, she began to weave the long stems and twigs together to form a circlet.

'It must be Spring...' he sniggered, 'looks like you caught the nest-building bug.'

Erica was determined not to let Simon spoil her day. 'At least I'm dressed for a pagan festival.' She glanced, disdainfully, at his pinstripe suit.

'I'm expecting a photographer,' he drawled. 'We don't want to end up in the tabloid press looking like village idiots, we have to have decorum.'

'Don't worry,' Erica replied, tartly, 'I'll keep out of the picture.' She valued her anonymity. Her photo had already appeared in the local paper on the day of the election count, and once was enough.

'I'm also discussing a fundraising idea with Rodney, beforehand,' Simon continued.

She had only met the Reverend Radpole once, at the count. Her first impression had not been favourable. 'I think I'll leave you to it.' She was happy to have the excuse to enjoy the celebrations without Simon.

No words were exchanged until they arrived in Witchbury. Her husband ploughed past adults and children milling on the Green and around the Village Hall. 'Try to look happy,' he said, forcing a grin.

Simon became annoyed. He struggled to find a place to park and eventually squeezed onto a muddy grass verge.

They walked back without talking. Simon threw well-practiced smiles to half recognised faces. They caught sight of the Reverend in the distance, and he strode off announcing to Erica that he would catch up with her later.

Erica breathed a deep sigh. Sometimes Simon was so suffocating, so stifling. The Spring air was perfumed with the scent of wildflowers and grasses. The fragrance of mayflowers pervaded her senses. Suddenly, Erica felt free. She meandered past the village shops and cottages and looked around in amazement. Overnight, the street had been transformed. Almost all the buildings were now draped in red and white streamers. The buildings along Silver Street huddled together in a comfortable jumble. It struck her it was as though they had just tumbled out from a box of toys belonging to the child. She was not surprised to discover the one remaining un-festooned facade belonged to the greengrocer.

From all five of the villages that shared the hidden Dorset valley, three generations had gathered outside the inn. Scattered along the intended route of the procession, families and friends stood in small groups. She positioned herself on the narrow pavement on the bridge over the Awen. Her view, there, would remain unobstructed.

It was as if the whole neighbourhood had summoned its combined will to banish the remnants of winter overnight. Erica had almost forgotten how clear the air could be. It was her first Spring in Dorset for over twenty-five years. Although she had the sense of returning home, it was as if she were seeing it all for the first time. Across the sky, clouds scudded like the sails of white galleons over a cerulean sea. Newly opened leaves of mature oaks and beeches once more had burst into life, covering the rolling hillsides in a green tint.

She closed her eyes and held her breath. A sense of optimism welled up inside her. Like the open landscape that lay in front, the rest of her life was there to be explored.

In south London, it would have been different. In the city, any celebration of the arrival of Spring would have been out of place, but here, the incessant traffic was replaced by the burble of the waters of the Awen and in the breath of the wind in the Oakenland. Here she heard echoes - voices of time, which spoke to her. Here she felt a sense of continuity, stretching back over thousands of years - a connection of the present with the past.

Somehow, the fabric of the village had combined with the landscape to make a setting close to perfection. Each colour, each form, each element contributed to make a whole. With any feature missing from its rightful place, the portrait would be incomplete.

She gazed over the parapet down at the fast-flowing waters. The surface lay only a few inches below the level of the top of the shallow arch. Near the bank, the clear water sparkled and bubbled over the pebbles on the riverbed. The rushing and gurgling completed the scene more fittingly than any musical score.

No longer surrounded by the chaos of the city, she could listen to her own thoughts, as clear as the melody of the river. Below her, a stout stick floated on the water. Brought to a halt against the buttress of the bridge, it seemed to be waiting for the current to break it free and send it on its way.

A familiar guffaw broke her reverie. It was Simon. He and the Reverend now stood together on the opposite side of the bridge. In his grey pinstripes, her husband looked so out of place. She and Simon were only a few yards apart, yet every pace between them now seemed to be a mile.

Suddenly, the slow beat of a bass drum shook her ribcage and Erica reached up to her heart. As her hand met the interlocking coils of the brooch, it felt hot to the touch.

CHAPTER 2
The Awakening

STARTING WITH A TINGLE in her fingers - a sensation entered her body. She felt its presence outside and within - the force that guides all creation, the power that makes the rivers flow and the flowers bloom. Once more, she looked about her at the hills, the trees and the grassy heath, and in the valley below, the fresh growth of corn pushed through the warming earth.

A mile away, the slow toll of St Michael's Tenor Bell rang clear. Then, the lighter tone of twelve strikes from the church clock called out in accompaniment.

'Osser... Osser... Osser...'

The cries brought her attention back to the Green. 'At last,' she thought. As though pent up aggression which had been kept bottled up for a whole year had been released, a huge roar broke out.

To remain an onlooker did not do justice to the force that had drawn her there. A desire took over, the opportunity at last to shout out the word at the top of her voice. 'Osser... Osser... Osser!'

In front of the Green Man, rowdy farmhands parted to allow a path for the pageant to move forward. One by one, the members of the procession came into view. A line of six figures in masks and cloaked heads emerged through the arch of the inn. They wore red capes with hoods of dark green. Leather masks hid their faces. From long flowing earth-red robes branches of oak and hawthorn hung. Clusters of bells jangled from their light green leggings. Some rattled loud wooden clappers.

A slow beat of rough music rang out and the crowd began to stomp on the cobbles.

Thump. Thump. Thump.

The bass beat pounded in the pit of her stomach. A red and yellow jester's hat shook to and fro. It was a few seconds before she realised that the drummer was the small man, she had seen in the library. He was dressed as the fool and marched wherever the spirit took him. The drum was as broad as he was tall. He struck out the primitive beat with a huge wooden flat spoon. He had to lean back in order that the drum did not snag the ground and send him skywards, rolling him over the top.

With cheers and catcalls, the mob spurred on the procession. Chaotic banging of metal and frantic clapping of wood heralded the long ragged conga. Like some ragbag dragon, rudely awoken from its midday slumbers, it snaked its way through the crowd.

A surge of exhilaration ran through her. In Erica's eyes the good-humoured ribaldry hid, not far below the surface, the thrill of a darker side. The crowd bayed and jeered, as though they were about to confront the devil incarnate.

To a crescendo of drums, a grotesque figure in animal skins emerged from a fanfare of fire. Erica's pulse locked into the tempo. She let out a shriek. Upon its head, were huge horns. Half man, half Horned Beast, it danced wildly. Behind, weaving through the crowd and echoing each twist and turn of the horned figure's every movement, came the six figures dressed in hoods.

At the rear, a gang of a dozen excited small lads goaded the procession with sticks. The drummer tried to scare them off by charging at them. He hit his drum louder still. They ran screaming, only to return and taunt even more.

This wild assemblage made its advance out of the throng toward the bridge. As the cacophony approached, the boom of the drum vibrated inside her. The beat overlaid and transcended everything - an incessant archaic pulse. Erica found her focus drawn by one thing alone, the figure at the front - the Horned Beast.

The Beast's grey straggly beard and long flowing locks shook as the masculine body lurched and lunged from side to side.

Erica was transfixed. Now she was no longer an observer, she had become a full participant. A cocktail of emotions welled up inside her - joy and exhilaration mixed with a sense of menace.

The Beast headed toward her, its eyes glowed translucent blood red.

The stare ignited a fire that started to burn deep inside her. Recklessly, again she joined in the shout. 'Osser, Osser…' She felt the power of the word envelope her.

The Beast reached the bridge. Held high in the air by the Beast, something turned, something twisted. White fangs shot from its mouth -hisssssssss.

Erica screamed - a snake!

The Horned Beast waved a torc - a circular band of twisted silver. The snake's head entered the silver ring of the torc. Its tongue lashed out. The Beast headed toward her, the pulsating rhythm rooted Erica to the spot. She stared up at the grotesque face and gasped. Now it stood, head and shoulders above her, and she was within its grasp. She felt possessed and heard a voice shout - 'Give, give!'

Erica grabbed at the brooch and held it tight against her heart.

A black veil suddenly shrouded the sun. Through a narrow slit in the cloud, a sun-shaft united her to the Beast. Deep furrows pitted its grotesque face, yet still she found herself drawn, as though her only destiny was to submit to its earthy power.

Erica's body gyrated. A surging current rushed through her veins. The Beast bucked and writhed. She felt its power. The raging creature was out of control. It lurched and lunged towards her with a ferocious strength. A latent force deep within awoke and welled up inside her. It rose up her spine. Erica shook uncontrollably. She had become its prey, the object of its desire - the chosen one.

Inside her head, the voice demanded of her again, 'Give… give.'

She held the bronze brooch tight, as though that were the only thing between her and another world. A raging heat exploded and burnt. Her fist clenched tighter around the hot bronze. A sting penetrated her finger. She cried out in shock. Framed against the threatening sky, the silhouette of the Beast stood menacingly above - the red-eyed stare etched itself into her being. The noise of the crowd and the drums merged into one one.

In the background, she heard a sweeter voice - as if the swift waters were calling to her.

Reluctantly, the Horned Beast turned away.

Released from the spell, she fell backwards. Her legs buckled. The base of her spine hit the top of the low parapet. For a moment that seemed to be outside time, she was pitched into a swirling vortex.

CHAPTER 3

The Rescue

ERICA GRABBED THE STONE parapet and managed to bring herself to an unsteady halt.

Her floral crown had flown into the air and fallen to land upon the silver surface of the water below. She twisted around to watch the strong current carry it along until it came to rest, impaled upon the stick, held there earlier by the buttress.

Merged with the thick haze of the noise of rushing water, Erica heard the soft sound of the woman's words clear and calm.

'You all right, my love?'

The voice remained disconnected, as though it was the river itself speaking. Erica felt a supportive arm around her shoulder. The reality of the physical touch of another person brought her back from the threshold.

The stick and crown were borne together through the centre arch of the bridge. 'That's an omen,' the soft voice said, 'she's carried you off.'

Erica found herself unable to utter a word of response. She blinked and tried to make sense of the picture in front of her. The dark cloud lifted and the scene became bathed in soft shadow. She held on to the arm, and turned towards her unidentified helper.

'How are you feeling?' The stranger stood above her. The sun shone from behind, and formed a halo of light around her blonde hair.

'What happened?' Erica held onto the woman's arm.

'You'll be all right.' She spoke in reassuring tones. 'You had an attack of the shakes. I thought for a moment you were having a fit.'

'I'm not epileptic or anything…' Her hurried apology sounded pathetic to her own ears. Erica glanced down at herself. She felt physically numb. How ludicrous she must look, slouched against the wall.

'You just went a little dizzy.' The woman gave a kindly smile.

Erica tried to push herself up but slumped back breathlessly.

An arm clasped her waist and slowly, the woman guided her to sit on the parapet. 'Just take it easy for a few seconds and you'll be fine.' The stranger steadied her. 'Stay sitting here for a bit until things have died down.' A group of noisy farmhands passed by, and she held Erica's shoulder.

Erica smiled an acknowledgement. 'What happened?' she asked again, perplexed.

'You had a bit of a turn. Take some deep breaths.'

Erica gulped in some air. The village boys were still goading the tail end of the procession. They screamed and shouted as they dipped and skipped over the bridge. To Erica, their voices now seemed removed and distant. The parade continued on its way and snaked-off through the gate, up the muddy path across the field toward the Oakenland and the Hill.

'Better now?' asked the woman.

Erica gave an anxious nod. Surely, the whole world must be looking at her. She gazed around but everyone, except her rescuer, seemed oblivious to her plight.

'My name's Vicky Fellows.' The woman flashed a friendly beam.

'Eric…ca… Janus,' came her hesitant response as she studied Vicky's face. She judged her to be about the same age as herself. Vicky had the beginnings of wrinkles around her eyes, a face full of character. Vicky had come from nowhere to be in the right place at the right time. 'You're very kind…' Shouts drowned Erica's words and she tried to stand.

'Careful.' Vicky held on to her arm and eased her back to sit on the low wall, once more. They waited for the remainder of the crowd to disperse. When the noise had died down, Vicky whispered in her local drawl, 'It can get pretty scary, can't it?'

Erica became aware she had been holding onto Vicky's arm and let go. 'I do beg your pardon.'

'I don't mind, it's safer,' Vicky assured her. 'Things can get a bit rowdy. Best to take time out.'

Gradually, Erica's senses heightened. She turned to look over her shoulder down to the swiftly flowing river below. There was now no sign of the May crown. 'I thought I was going to end up in there.'

'You wouldn't be the first one. You almost went the same way as your May blossom.'

'Did you see what happened to my crown? It floated off…' Erica peered again over the parapet.

'Don't worry about that now. Janus did you say?' A hint of recognition hit the stranger's face. 'Aren't you the wife of our new MP? I saw your picture in the local paper.'

Erica looked around. Where was Simon? 'The night of the election result, that's right,' Erica nodded. 'I came here with my husband, but he seems to have disappeared.'

The swell in the crowd subsided and, this time guided by Vicky, Erica stood up. She glanced around, trying to regain her bearings. Opposite, a group of middle-aged women had reached various pitches of excitability. Erica recognised a red-faced Beebee. Next to her was a diminutive woman in neat tweeds. They briefly stared across and Erica turned away, feeling uncomfortable at being seen at a disadvantage.

Vicky gave them a token wave. 'What are you going to do now?' she asked. 'Will you carry on up the Hill?'

'I'll wait here for a bit.' She wanted to follow the revellers but Erica felt giddy. 'I need to get my breath back.'

'I think we can say the show's over now here. Would you like a lift?' Vicky offered. 'You're in Upper Melbury aren't you?' continued Vicky. 'It's on my way.'

Given the current state of play with Simon, Erica did not refuse. 'If it's no trouble…' Erica smiled. 'My husband can make his own way home. He has the car. I'll text him.'

Vicky chirped. 'Just give me a minute.'

Erica felt she had found a kindred spirit in Vicky. The villagers were welcoming enough, but most seemed to stay at arm's length. To her, many of the locals appeared to be formal and distant. Having the tag of MP's wife didn't help. In over two months, she had yet to meet anyone with whom she could feel fully at ease. Perhaps she had expected village life to be cosier. She knew most villagers would always view her as an outsider.

For nearly twenty years, she had allowed herself to be cloaked in anonymity in the soulless suburbs of south London. This, at times, had been both an asset and an annoyance, according to circumstance. She had become accustomed to it, but it had caused her spirits to be dulled. Underneath, she had always been aware of feeling life should be better.

The morning she had woken to the news that Simon might have a chance to stand for Wessex South, the realisation had hit her. She had been blind to it for so long - only by leaving London could she regain her soul. Perhaps she had refused to think about it before, for the same reason a prisoner might wish to avoid thinking of freedom, until a chance of escape presented itself.

By moving to Dorset, she hoped to find a greater sense of belonging, and to live somewhere she could call home. Whether it was an idealistic notion, she had yet to discover. Having friends locally would be one thing that would help. A masculine growl brought her out of her reverie.

'Shall I find your husband for you?'

Flustered, she jumped to her feet, brushed herself down with her hands and nervously tidied her hair. It was the Reverend.

He gestured toward the pub. 'Isn't that him with that young lady?'

It took a few seconds before Erica homed in on Simon in his dark grey suit. He stood laughing and joking with a woman in combat fatigues. They were at the doorway to the lounge bar. Erica could not avoid herself automatically jumping to Simon's defence. 'It must be someone from the press.'

Radpole grimaced. 'I could pop over to the pub, it's no trouble. They do let me in there, you know.' He snorted a stifled chuckle.

'It's fine thank you Reverend, and I'm perfectly ok now… someone's offered…' Erica spun around. 'Oh, she's gone…'

The Reverend gestured across to the group of women on the other side of the road. 'Vicky is over with my ladies.'

His ladies… how patronising to call them *his* ladies. Erica tried to catch Vicky's attention.

'Magnificent…' The declaration made Erica jump. 'Symmetrical, well balanced, fascinating. You don't mind if I take a closer look, do you… '

Slightly thrown, Erica gave a sigh of recognition - the Reverend was admiring her brooch.

'However did you come by it?'

'My daughter gave it to me this morning…' she stammered. 'The design is rather unusual.'

'Look where you're going, young man!' Radpole shouted and steadied her against his body. One of the rougher types, slightly the worse for drink, had stumbled into Erica and jolted her forward.

The ruddy-faced oaf threw a curse at the Reverend. 'She your bit on the side, Hot Rod?'

Vicky came scurrying back. 'Really,' she scowled, 'some people have no manners. You were in good hands with Rodney, though.'

Erica composed herself and attempted a smile and thanked the Reverend. 'We have met before.'

'Indeed, we have, Mrs Janus, the night of the count.' He nodded, toward her dress, enthusiastically. 'What a charming outfit you have on, you're the Queen of the May, I'm sure.'

'Unfortunately…' she glanced once more over the parapet, '…I lost my crown.'

'How inopportune,' the Reverend declared. 'Naturally, we'll be seeing you at the May Day service tomorrow…'

It was almost an order.

Vicky responded on Erica's behalf. 'I'm looking forward to it, Rodney.' She turned to her new companion. 'I've offered Mrs Janus a lift.'

The Reverend beamed. 'See you tomorrow, both of you.'

The two of them had set off along the narrow pavement toward Silver Street when they heard a shout. They turned to see the Reverend stoop to retrieve something from off the ground. 'Mrs Janus, wait…' He hurried toward them. 'Allow me.'

'The brooch,' Erica gasped. 'Reverend, it's lucky you saw it. It must have fallen off in the fracas.'

'Your daughter would have been upset if you'd lost it.' He shuffled closer as he fastened it to her red stole. 'It suits you. I've never seen anything like it, it's quite beautiful. Oh, you've pricked yourself.'

A drop of blood dribbled from her finger. Erica realised it must have been the pin. 'It's nothing, it happened when the Horned Monster…' She tailed off feeling embarrassed.

Radpole fussed over Erica, and Vicky produced a handkerchief. 'Thank you, Rodney,' interjected Vicky, and took Erica once more by the arm, 'we'll be all right now.'

'If you're sure…' He beamed at them both. 'See you tomorrow.'

When they were a few yards down the street Vicky turned to Erica to study the brooch. 'May I see?'

Erica handed it to her. 'It was a spur of the moment thing this morning. Sarah did warn me but I hadn't realised the pin was quite so loose.'

'It's certainly very unusual.' Vicky passed it back. 'Sam, my Uncle, could take a look at it for you. He has the antique shop.'

Erica put it back in the pouch in her handbag. 'I'll suggest it to Sarah.' She took Vicky's arm and they walked along the narrow pavement. The crowds were breaking up and moving on. 'Vicky, you seem to know the Reverend quite well.'

Vicky looked at her, warily. 'He's been our vicar for ten years. I do the church flowers every Sunday, so naturally we've developed a friendship.'

'Perhaps I'm being overly sensitive…' Erica paused. 'I hope you won't mind me saying, but for a man of the cloth, he does come over a little bit errrm…over attentive.'

'I'm used to his ways.' Vicky was curt. 'It's all perfectly innocent.'

'I'm sure,' Erica nodded in response. 'What was it that yob called him?'

'Oh that… Rodney has an old BSA, that's all, a hangover from the sixties. He used to be a bit of a rocker.'

Erica gave a sigh of acknowledgement. 'You must tell me more about him sometime. Being a newcomer, I still feel a bit of an outsider.'

'After confronting the Horny Monster, you're well initiated,' Vicky looked rather stern.

Erica chuckled. 'I trust you're not referring to the Reverend Hot Rod?'

They laughed.

CHAPTER 4
The Way of the Wolf

'WHERE'S THAT DAMN PHOTOGRAPHER...' Twelve o'clock struck and Simon was on the phone to *the Echo*. 'If they don't bloody well show up soon, it'll be all over!'

Simon had fixed on seeing the event as a photo opportunity, and nothing was going to divert him. George, the editor, had been unenthusiastic and had muttered some excuse about 'not wanting to go against local tradition', but in the end, he had reluctantly agreed to send someone.

Simon had been pleased that his fundraising idea for the church had gone down so well with the Reverend. They had then talked about cricket, and to top it all, Rodney had invited Simon to play in the village team for the new season. However, Simon now had other things on his mind. With the arrival of the procession on the bridge, and the press nowhere in sight, Simon was in a pique of frustration.

From the open gate, spectators strung out in two lines to mark the route up toward the Oakenland. Simon entered the field and tried to keep up with the procession by sidling alongside. With bangs of the huge drum in the MP's ear, the jester thwarted his efforts to get close.

Didn't he know who he was – 'I'm Simon Janus, the Right Honourable Member for Wessex South,' he shouted. 'Damn idiot...' Simon uttered, under his breath. 'Bombastic little man.'

He had all but given up hope of the press, when a girl in combat fatigues and laden with camera gear came running through the gateway. 'About time …' Simon barked. For a few seconds, the jester had become preoccupied with chasing away the gang at the rear. He took his chance. 'Come on…' he shouted and grabbed the press-girl by the arm. They charged up the grassy slope.

The press-girl crouched down and aimed the lens up the nostrils of Simon and the Monster. A quick fire round from her flashgun caused the Monster to lunge toward the MP.

Simon ducked.

The Beast's eyes glared. The diminutive jester ran up with an explosion of indignant snorts. The veins on his bulbous nose glowed purple. He waved his oversized stick and banged his drum with fury.

Simon conducted a tactical retreat behind the press-girl. 'Bloody hell…' he fumed.

The jester made a snatch at the camera. The press-girl swung out with her equipment bag and dented the jester's cap.

She and Simon escaped backwards down the slope, with the jester in hot pursuit. The small man stumbled and the bass drum, with him attached, rolled down the hill toward them. The camera flashed. The crowd swarmed around them like angry wasps. Their escape was blocked.

The self-propelled drummer crashed into the press-girl. Her backside bumped into Simon's stomach. Simon fell rearwards to land on his backside in a cowpat. The press-girl ended up in a tousled heap on top.

'Grummmfff…' Simon puffed. He lay winded, sprawled in the mud. A cacophony of catcalls from the crowd drowned Simon's ensuing profanities.

The pair grabbed hold of each other as they tried to avoid being trampled under foot. The drum continued to roll down the slope with the jester attached.

'Somehow,' the press-girl gave a sardonic smirk, 'I get the feeling we're not welcome.' From her vantage point mounted on top of the MP, she chose to defy the barrage of jeers and grabbed her camera. 'Yeh right on… fantastic…' She fired off expletives, faster than shots from the flashgun. Simon's stout frame provided a dramatic angle on the action.

'Hey, I'm not a bloody tripod you know…' Simon remonstrated.

The press-girl crawled over Simon, and continued with the shoot.

The bass drum came to a halt, with the jester strapped beneath it. After a few seconds of dizzy disorientation, the jester managed to propel himself to his feet. His bow-legged gait strained once more under the weight of the drum. He looked around and snarled at them, then turned and staggered off to chase after the tail-enders.

'Bit of a disaster I'm afraid.' Simon was still flat out as he looked bewildered at the press-girl on top of him.

'Bloody great shoot, a bit of action at last…'

Impressed by her spirit, Simon puffed, 'A touch lively, I agree.'

Simon's understatement brought a grin to her lips. 'There's me expecting a dreary old shoot, full of boring old farts.' She continued, in upbeat mode, 'I should've been a war correspondent.'

He stared in beleaguered disbelief at the surrounding sea of mud. 'It's the bloody trenches here all right,' he gasped.

She was not the type he normally would have found appealing. Strands of bright copper hair, tied up with assorted pink and green thread, jutted out from under her baseball cap. Camouflage gear, fatigues and Doc Martens were not really his thing. Under different circumstances, she would have fallen somewhere between 'bitch' and 'butch' in Simon's formbook. However, to seek advantage out of adversity is second nature to a politician. Simon was not only a MP but also an alpha male. Unexpected full body contact with the youthful female journalist sparked a hormone burst that was simply irrepressible. A switch tripped deep within his primeval cortex. The insult to his dignity transformed itself miraculously into a divine gift.

The press-girl stood up, gazed at the be-mudded Simon, and turned her mind to his plight. With the air of a salvage contractor about to remove a beached whale, she cocked her cap, raised an eyebrow, and scratched her temple. 'Catch hold...' she shouted, and threw down the thick shoulder strap from her kit bag.

With a series of shrieks from the press-girl and a good deal of grunting from Simon, the stranded MP was winched to his feet. 'Thanks...' Simon nodded, and wheezed as he clambered up, 'so, did you get it?'

The press-girl looked thrown. 'What was that, sorry?'

'Did you get it? Me and that crazy... horny... thing...' Simon spluttered.

The press-girl nodded. 'I got it, alright.' The press-girl held up her arms to fend off a farmhand who came hurtling toward them. She deftly dealt with the drunken oaf to dispatch him off down the steep hill. She put the camera back in her bag, before turning with a look of satisfaction of a job well done.

Simon looked up with relief. 'No one told me it was going to be like this.' He said, gruffly. 'Worked out a touch tougher than I thought.' A whiff of a heady scent wafted up his nostrils and made his nose-hairs twitch. 'Nice perfume,' he growled.

'And you...' She glanced pointedly at the large brown patch on the rear of his trousers.

He twisted around. 'This photo had better bloody be worth it, after all this.' The tone of his voice harboured a level of undisguised misgiving.

The press-girl dived into one of her many pockets, 'No problem, hold on...' She pulled out a large disposable lens cloth. 'Keep still.' She squatted down and managed to wipe off the worst of the cowpat from Simon's trousers.

'You don't have to do this, you know.' Simon was secretly enjoying the special treatment.

She looked up at him from her crouching position. 'No worries... all part of the service,' she chirped back.

She crouched in front of him and he stared in disbelief at her assortment of straps, zippers and camera gear. She noticed his gaze. 'I've come well equipped.'

Unavoidably, he peered down the front of her jerkin. 'So you have,' he said.

She brushed off the remains of the brown gunge as best she could.

Falling into a pile of cow dung would have been enough to cool any red-blooded male's ardour. Simon however, was not easily thwarted. The situation had already afforded a degree of unbridled intimacy. An envoy from the local press at his feet - what more could he ask for? He held out a helping hand. She took it.

'Pleased you made it.' Simon said and nodded at her combat gear, 'You came prepared.' He noticed her return a sceptical eye over his pinstriped suit. 'Dressed up a touch for the photograph,' he quipped. 'By the way, I'm Simon Janus.'

'Phew, just as well you are, or back at base my name would be mud.'

'I presume your name isn't really Miss Mud?' Simon jibed.

'Sorry...' She held out her dirt-stained hand. 'Beth Frank, pleased to meet you, I must be starting to think like a journalist - apt turn of phrase in the circumstance...mud...'

As Simon took her hand, he gave her an ingratiating look and studied her from head to foot, as though he were a farmer scrutinizing a prize heifer. An inane grin fell over his face. The notion had struck him that only he could find benefit from landing in a pile of crap. That cowpat could be worth its weight in gold.

The press-girl grinned back. 'You have to see the funny side.'

'Funny side?' he echoed and craned his neck to inspect his rear. 'Listen, I don't want to be on my backside on the front page - it's not the most flattering of angles.'

She looked around her at the mud bath. 'I don't do flattery, I do drama.'

Simon could tell her voice was charged with adrenalin and he raised his eyebrows. 'You weren't disappointed with the shoot then?'

'No way... brilliant shoot... Should have some good stuff.'

The noise from the crowd died down a little. Simon conjectured she had become ignited by the thrill of the foray, and felt sure the young woman would not refuse lunch. It was time for the charm offensive. The opportunity of entertaining a woman half his age buoyed Simon's spirits, and he had now become blind to her eccentrically modern appearance. 'Come on, let's get out of here.' He extended his arm around her shoulder and ushered her back through the gate to the relative calm of the other side of the bridge.

Circuitry, deep within the primal brain of the male, once stimulated is not so easy to shut down. Simon had become temporarily oblivious to the existence of anyone else. All others were for the present, out of his field of view, and out of his mind.

He looked down at her mud stained fatigues. 'Now, it's my turn.'

'It's only a bit of dried dirt,' she insisted, 'no worries.'

'My pleasure.' Simon had none of it and tried to slap her thigh. The cloud of ensuing dust caused him to cough. 'Sorry about that, do excuse me,' he spluttered. Oblivious to his overt hands-on, preening ritual, he re-focussed on his immediate goal. 'Right, lunch.' His zeal unimpaired, they strode toward the pub.

She stared up at the many-fingered signpost at the junction of Silver Street and looked bemused. 'I almost missed the bash. Haven't got a clue where I am.'

'You're new to the newspaper…' Simon had the sense she was easy prey. 'You'll soon get to know your way around.'

'Moved to Dorchester from London a few days ago. This is my first assignment down here. I'm not used to these narrow roads. They're like a ruddy rabbit warren. I've no idea how I got here. Everywhere has such weird names.'

'I assume George sent you.' Simon dropped the name of the editor with an air intended to convey they were long-standing friends.

'What's George gonna say when I tell him I ended up rolling on top of you,' she said.

Simon was wary. 'I don't think he would approve,' he stuttered.

She knew the editor had only spoken to Simon once, on the phone. 'I can hack a bit of rough and tumble, but George didn't tell me it was going to be a bloody battleground.' She nodded back to the field where, in the distance, the procession was still wending its way up the muddy hill. 'What the hell was that all about anyway?'

'Nothing to worry about, just some damn silly local superstition.'

'Superstition?' she asked, keenly.

'Some stupid thing about no publicity.'

She was taken aback. 'Now you bloody tell me! So can we still use the pictures?'

'It's about time this lot moved into the twenty-first century. It's one of my roles to get them there. Thought the hooha might give the story an edge but didn't quite expect a re-enactment of the Somme.' Simon gestured toward the Green Man. 'I'll tell you over lunch.'

'I don't know if there's time before my next project.' She threw him a demure look.

Simon judged the press-girl's tone to be a taunt. 'A project am I?' he joked. 'Quick snack, then.'

'I guess I could manage that,' she agreed.

He could detect the making of a win-win situation. Simon considered what he might offer her - a valuable contact inside parliament, at least, for as long as she might be useful to him. Moreover, what would he win - an insider in the local press and, naturally, whatever else there might be up for grabs... Of course, there may be dangers, but that was half the fun. She was harmless enough. 'After all,' he told himself, '*the Wessex Echo* is not exactly the tabloid press.' He permitted himself the pleasure of a self-satisfied smirk. Simon noticed Beth return a restrained grin. Was she playing to his thoughts?

Simon viewed life as a series of missions. Occasionally, some were God-given - there was no question about it, this one was ordained. In the distance, he was vaguely aware of the Reverend and Erica on the bridge, but they had for now become irrelevant. To Simon, this bird had turned into fair game - the quarry in his sights was now the centre of his attention and he would dedicate himself to bagging a kill.

Simon guided her through the remains of the crowd, and toward the entrance to the lounge. He opened the door and beckoned her through. The pub was packed. 'No worries, we can squeeze in, I know the landlord.' He shepherded her into the low-beamed room and they worked their way to the bar. Simon moved up closer to her to take advantage of the opportunity the crowded room offered. 'You must have a tremendously interesting job.' He flattered.

'Not half as interesting as yours,' she replied, straining her voice over the clamour.

'Sitting through all those back bench committees can be very dull, you know. People think it's glamorous, but it's bloody boring most of the time. What'll you have?'

'White wine…' she answered, and they manoeuvred through the unruly mob crowding the bar.

Simon called across the counter, 'Jerry, a bottle of Chardonnay,' and added, 'with a jug of iced water.'

The landlord looked harassed, but at the sight of the MP he moved over to him. 'Mr Janus, I've got something for you.' From under the counter, he handed over a black briefcase. 'The blond lad said you would be expecting it.'

'Ahh yes.' Simon placed it carefully by his side. 'This lady might do an article on your pub if you play your cards right.'

The landlord looked sceptically at Simon's mud spattered face and nodded in the direction of the procession. 'Looks like you discovered, they don't like publicity.'

'Natives were a touch hostile. Anyone would think taking a few snaps was going to take away their souls.'

Simon's aside had no effect on the landlord. 'People like things just as they are. Folk don't go in for change'

'Quick, take that.' Simon thrust the bag into Beth's hands. 'I'll bring the tray.'

Two seats had become vacant near the log fire and they hurried over. 'Hold on…' she took a paper napkin off the table and placed it on the chair.

Simon sat on the napkin and poured out two glasses. 'Iced water,' he confirmed.

She took a napkin, dipped it in the jug and dabbed the dirt from his brow. 'Here's mud in your eye,' she quipped. They raised their glasses.

Simon noticed her glance at his case. 'Just a present,' he stated.

'So… why don't they go in for publicity?' she asked, changing tack.

'Some old mumbo-jumbo,' he huffed.

She looked serious. 'Are we going to be able to run the picture?'

'It'll all add spice. I'll clear it through, no worries. After all, your editor sent you, didn't he.'

She handed Simon her business card.

He studied it and took the opportunity to call her by her first name. 'So Beth, I see you're based in Dorchester…'

'Only been there for a week or so.' She looked around the crowded bar. 'Is this your local?'

'Saturday lunchtimes after golf, mostly… Tell me, do you think we'll make the front page?'

Beth had a mischievous twinkle. 'It might achieve quite an impact.'

'Hmmm…' Simon grunted, warily, 'any good ideas for a caption?'

She thought for a moment, and then scribbled on the beer mat.

Simon read it out. 'Janus Joins Monster Mash Mêlée!' He raised an eybrow. 'This is Dorset not the Dordogne, Mêlée's a bit Franglais, but it does have a certain *je ne sais quoi*.'

'Don't you mean Janus *sais quoi*?' Beth quipped.

'*Touché mon amie*,' Simon grinned. 'So tell me about your job, do you enjoy it?'

'It keeps me on the streets, you know.'

Beth's banter relaxed him another notch. He was warming to her. A technique picked up from his days in marketing was to break things down into achievable chunks.

Stage one: establish rapport.

Stage two: make her see it was in her interests to get to know him.

Stage three: exploit the opportunity.

Onward to stage two of the mission…

Unbeknown to Simon, Beth was also on a mission. She was far from the young and hapless girl he had casually assumed her to be. Young yes, twenty-three and inexperienced perhaps. She had left university with a First Class in politics from Cambridge the previous summer, however her assumed pretence of innocence was but a Trojan Horse. She took pleasure in seeing he was willing to believe that he was the one making the running. If she had not already thought of the idea herself, she would have seen it as patronising when the editor suggested that getting to know the MP might be beneficial to her prospects. George had talked about him as though he was a rising star and who could tell what post the politician might aspire to. It would indeed suit her very well, to get to know the honourable Simon Janus.

They had reached the end of the seafood salad, before Simon began to wonder whether there might be more to Beth than met the eye. 'So what time's your next project?' Simon made it sound as though whatever else there may be, it could only be of trivial importance.

'It can wait till tomorrow,' she said emphatically.

He was waiting for that opening. He had suspected there had never been another assignment. Simon was cottoning on to Beth's ways, and enjoyed playing along. 'That's very noble of you, to work Sundays I mean.'

'Being freelance, the course of events dictates what I do.' She took a sip of her wine. 'I don't always do what I am told, Mr Janus,' she added.

'You have a great deal of freedom. If I'm not present for a division vote,' he added, 'then I've the whip to think about, you know.'

'I've heard MP's go in for discipline…' she said, laconically.

They were reaching the end of the Chardonnay and unconscious speculations began to surface in his mind… just how much more might be hidden under the combat gear. 'So what else do you do in your spare time?' Simon sometimes had the gift, by sheer tone alone, of making the most banal phrase carry immense nuance of meaning.

She raised an eyebrow. 'This and that.'

'This and that?' he queried.

'One of my interests is first editions. I have a Malthus.'

'However did you come by that?' Simon was impressed.

'My father left it to me.' This was a lie. Her research on Simon had been thorough; she had borrowed the book, as a result from a tip-off from a journalist friend, in case she needed bait.

'That's amazing, that you have one. A first edition,' Simon clarified.

'My father died in my teens,' she said in a matter of fact tone. This was not a lie.

He sympathised. 'Sorry to hear that.'

'I got over it. It made me more independent and more determined, probably.'

'I can understand that.' Simon moved into overdrive. 'I would love to see your Malthus.'

'I'd be happy to show it to you.'

The MP was hooked and too absorbed by his own agenda to detect Beth's interest in Malthus could be anything other than sheer coincidence. He reached down to pick up the padded briefcase and made to get ready.

'So what's in the case?' she queried again.

'A laptop.'

'Does Jerry sell computers from under the counter?' she asked.

'I bought it from a young lad I met in here last week. He left it for me to collect, all perfectly legit. Perhaps I'd better go home first, and change out of these trousers.' Simon shrugged.

'No need, they'll clean up easily enough, we'll do it at my place.'

'Well, if you're sure…' He was unable to avoid sounding eager.

She returned a wry grin.

He looked again at her business card. 'The Loft, The Brewery, Dorchester. Sounds interesting, drink up then.'

'They don't brew beer there any longer, but I do have a bottle of wine and a few canapés in the fridge.'

Simon licked his lips with the air of a slightly elderly Labrador having been promised a treat.

CHAPTER 5

The Prediction

'IT'S NOT FAR, I'M parked next to Sam's Emporium.'

'Sam is your uncle,' Erica confirmed.

Vicky nodded.

Erica had to remind herself that less than an hour ago they had not even met, and yet, to her, Vicky already felt like a trusted friend.

Cottages and shops lined each side of Silver Street. Oriels and bays punctuated the honey stone, which melted into washed out soft white facades. Roofs were swathed in sheets of slate and blankets of thatch. There was a harmony in the curious inevitability of how each form followed the other.

Erica gazed at the garlands of green, still amazed at the magical transformation that had taken place overnight. 'It's strange to see all this now, and yet no-one seemed to want to acknowledge the ceremony even existed, before today.'

'It's just second nature,' Vicky confirmed. 'Monday it'll all be back as normal.'

Erica nodded. 'I thought the silence over the festival odd at first, but after a week of knowing about the custom, it seems quite natural. Simon thinks it's just a load of hocus-pocus.'

'Folk had to keep quiet about the old religion.' Vicky's tone was serious. 'That's why the secrecy, especially for those taking part in the procession.'

The explanation left Erica thinking. 'I've read people were persecuted by the Church for their beliefs in the past, but surely, it doesn't happen any more, after all, the Reverend joined in too.'

Vicky nodded. 'He likes being centre stage.'

Erica paused at the one shop without bunting. Flaking purple woodwork told of better days. The roof stooped down at one end, from old age.

Vicky read Erica's thoughts. 'Matches her character quite well, don't you think?' she chuckled.

'Why doesn't Miss Bird join in?' Erica asked.

Vicky shrugged. 'She's a bit of an odd ball.'

The haphazard array of crates of fruit and vegetables piled precariously on the narrow pavement forced the companions to uncouple their arms and step off the kerb. 'These wouldn't last long in Streatham High Road,' Erica joked.

They gazed at Miss Bird's eccentric window display. A rogues' gallery of vegetables were set out like an identity parade, next to the largest and most mutated of which she had chalked the word 'organ'.

Erica looked at Vicky with a wry expression. 'Do you think she means organic?'

'Who knows,' Vicky spoke in hushed tones. 'I wouldn't take too much notice of her, Erica, she is about as twisted as one of her parsnips.'

A yellow, wizened face with screwed-up eyes, a pointed chin and thin, crooked lips peered out from the window and grimaced menacingly at them.

Erica and Vicky quickly went on their way. For several paces, they remained silent and then Vicky burst out. 'Do you think she heard me?'

'If you get served corkscrewed parsnips next time you are in her shop,' Erica chuckled, 'you'll know why.'

'I've nothing else planned for today. Care to come back for a coffee?' suggested Vicky.

Erica readily agreed. 'I'm free this afternoon. Sarah's gone to stay the night at her friend's.'

'How old's your daughter?' Vicky enquired.

'Seventeen tomorrow, she was born on my twenty-third birthday. Simon jibes he's never needed to give me another birthday present since.'

'Happy fortieth, are you celebrating tomorrow?'

'Your maths is too good, Vicky.' Erica paused. 'Simon and I don't go in for celebrations anymore, and Sarah prefers to be with other teenagers.'

'Hmm... tell me about it,' Vicky said ruefully, 'they like their freedom.'

'Apart from me acting as a taxi service, Sarah's quite independent - nevertheless, I worry whenever she's late, you know how it is...'

Vicky nodded. 'My boy, Will, he's nineteen and six foot tall. I've no idea where he is half the time, and it's probably best I don't.'

'Perhaps we should introduce the two of them...' suggested Erica, half in jest.

'I'm not so sure that would be such a good idea. Will is a good lad, but his name suits his nature, he is very self-willed.' Vicky chuckled, 'I expect they'll come across each other sooner or later, though.'

They approached a break in the line of the streetscape. Tucked into the gap was a small shop frontage. Over the door hung a signboard of deep blue and gold copperplate script – 'Antique Emporium' it announced, and under this, in modest capitals the name of the proprietor was printed, 'Samuel Haines.'

Erica peered in. In the murky shades of brown and grey she could make out strange artefacts - a stuffed armadillo, a bear, sculpture and jewellery. 'Wow, it's full of treasure.'

'It's a bit like Dr Who's Tardis inside, packed full of allsorts - quite a treasure chest. I'm always surprised how much Sam knows about the oddest things.' Vicky added, enthusiastically.

'Your uncle sounds a bit of a treasure himself...'

'He is. I always leave Morris here when I'm in the village. After all, it's something of an antique.' Vicky gazed proudly at the car. The Traveller's bottle green paintwork looked almost like new but, due to many layers of yacht varnish, the wood strips along each side had developed the same golden brown patina as one of Sam's walnut bureaus.

'Amazing, my mother had one just like this.' Erica stood back in admiration.

'It does have a touch of what one might call the distressed look about it, but then so do I, and after all, Morris is even older than me.' Vicky opened the passenger door. 'Jump in.'

Erica fell into the passenger's seat, and looked across to the neatly patched faded leather on the driver's side. For a split second, a delicate woman wearing a red hat and a white dress with small red polka dots sat at the wheel.

'Everything ok?' Vicky asked.

Erica blinked several times. 'Sorry, just daydreaming - for a second, I could picture my mother sitting there.' Erica nodded toward the steering wheel.

'I hope she can drive,' Vicky jested.

Erica laughed as she stroked the dashboard, 'This feels so familiar. Yet, it's been over twenty-five years.'

Vicky turned the ignition key. The engine spluttered to life. 'Morris knows the way home like a pet dog.'

'I'm not sure my Jet knows his way yet.'

'What sort is he?' Vicky enquired.

'… a black Labrador. So many new places to explore… Simon leaves dog walking to me. I don't mind, I love to go to the Oakenland and up on the Hill.'

Vicky glanced across at her. 'Maybe I could join you sometime?'

Erica sat back against the warmth of the old leather. 'That'd be great.' She held the chromium handle and wound down the window. The smell of fresh Spring grass mixed with the heady scent of cowslips rushed in and merged with the sun-warmed leather. The tepid breeze caressed her face and tossed her bronze hair against her neck. 'I could almost be a schoolgirl again.'

Vicky chuckled. 'I often regress to being seventeen.' She glanced down at her figure with a comic frown. 'I only wish my body did too.'

'I might take you up on that offer.' In the space of an hour, Erica already knew she had found a friend in Vicky.

The sun shone through the open window. The hawthorn hedges were alight with glistening white. The winding lane crept along the valley bottom, following the course of the river. As they drove, Erica caught the occasional glimpse of the sparkle of the Awen through the trees.

'Doesn't she look inviting?' Vicky said, reading Erica's thoughts.

Erica looked round at Vicky. 'Can I ask you a question… why do you refer to the river as female?'

'It's just a custom,' Vicky replied.

Erica gazed wistfully down into valley. The river unwound like a piece of decorative silver thread, discarded from an unwrapped gift. If there were a perfect present, she thought, it would surely be the Oakenland. The open wooded country that enveloped the Hill had become as treasured to her in two months as any object she had possessed.

Far off to the south, in the distance, the land gently rolled away to the English Channel, where the hills tumbled into the sea and formed cliffs of hidden fossils, and where as a child she had played.

Built by the Celts, rising above the green foliage of the Oakenland, lay the hill fort - the Hill as the locals called it. Remnants of old structures, monuments and earthworks littered the skyline.

The languid valley also held the Cauldron - a secret space hidden by the cliff that rose on three sides. It formed a flat-bottomed bowl in the landscape, about two hundred yards across. Near its centre stood the church, and hidden in the trees lay the Manse. Above, the hard limestone escarpment of Devil's Drop formed the east side of the Hill.

'There are so many strange features,' Erica commented.

'I took them all for granted when I was young.' Vicky glanced up at the summit where the giant Hell Stone poked up into the sky.

'What's that grass track?' Erica looked high on the side of the Hill.

'You mean the Cursus. Who knows what it was for... some say it is a guide for the spirits, a bit like Jacob's ladder in the Bible.'

'A pathway to heaven...' Erica whispered.

They travelled in contented silence for about a mile along the valley, until they climbed to where Cauldron Road turned off to the church and the Manse at Hobbs Cross. The square stone bell tower stood framed by the surrounding trees. The young foliage of the canopy provided a freshly painted canvas of beech, oak, birch, ash and hawthorn flower from a palette of delicate greens and creams. 'Much to my husband's irritation, this is where I picked the flowers for my crown this morning.' Then, Erica asked, 'Why do you think they built St Michael's down that dead end road?'

'I don't know for sure,' Vicky paused. 'There's the Portal.' She spoke the words with a degree of hushed reverence.

'The stone in Cauldron Field,' Erica confirmed.

'It's like the twin of the Altar on top of the Hill. They remind me of two halves of an apricot.'

Erica was fascinated. 'I wonder why one is at the top and one at the bottom.'

'If the Celts placed them there, they'd have had a reason...' Vicky looked thoughtful. 'The early Church took over most ancient sites. They built over standing stones and cut down the sacred oak groves, all in the name of the new religion.'

Erica guessed from her tone that this might be one of Vicky's pet subjects.

Vicky continued. 'The zealots wanted to usurp whatever spiritual energy was associated with the ancient pagan sites. By building near them, they thought it would help to destroy the old religion.'

Erica looked puzzled. 'So, why didn't they build on top of the Portal itself?'

'I expect they wanted to hedge their bets. Even the churchmen were probably superstitious about the old ways.'

'So why's it called the Portal?' Erica asked.

At first, Vicky did not answer then began to talk, haltingly. 'Entry to the Otherworld is within reach only at certain times in certain places, otherwise the spirit is lost...'

'The Otherworld?' Erica asked.

It's an entrance to a doorway of dreams,' Vicky added, and her eyes filled with tears.

Erica wanted to discover more but the subject seemed to be too upsetting for her friend.

They turned off the main road. The car chugged up the steep hill out of one valley and back down into the next hidden fold in the landscape toward the hamlets of Upper and Lower Melbury.

Erica changed the subject. 'I have to thank you again for what you did earlier at the bridge.'

Vicky had recovered and turned her head briefly toward Erica, 'No problem. So tell me, what do you think your husband made of the ceremony?'

'He would have preferred to spend the morning on the golf course, but he arranged to see some journalist to get his picture in the paper - it was the only reason he came.'

'I'm surprised they agreed to take the photo.'

'Simon just laughs it off as some silly superstition.'

'Perhaps he has a point, this place does need some new ideas.' After a few seconds, Vicky continued. 'Obviously, he's not planning to settle-down into anonymity, now he's won the seat?'

'With a majority of ninety-five?' Erica chuckled. 'He's the opposite from me. Simon enjoys courting controversy. He's a hard-nosed politician and says it gets him noticed. After the bye-election, media interest died down. Personally, I avoid the press like the plague.'

Vicky glanced across. 'What's it like being an MP's wife?'

Erica shrugged. 'We only see each other at weekends. Thinking about it,' Erica added, sardonically, 'I'm not so sure that's such a huge downside.'

'And the upsides?' Vicky enquired.

'For me,' Erica pointed enthusiastically out of the open window, 'living here.'

'Didn't your husband mind leaving London?' Vicky quizzed.

'He's still there five days a week… and he has his golf and cricket.'

'He should have a word with Rodney,' Vicky suggested.

'About the cricket team, you mean? He probably already has. They were talking together earlier. Simon has different needs from me. Now Sarah is older, we're both rediscovering our own interests.'

'At least you're still together.' Vicky had a rueful expression. An engraved oak sign swung gently in the breeze, and announced Four Winds - Bed and Breakfast. 'Here we are.'

Erica looked around in admiration. 'Your house looks charming.'

The cottage lay at the end of the terrace built in the local golden limestone. From openings set deep in the solid walls, shone leaded diamonds. They reflected the sunlight and animated the façade as they walked up the path. To Erica it felt like the sparkle in the eyes of a friendly face.

Vicky turned the key in the mortise of the dark oak panelled door. The hinges squeaked as it swung open and Vicky ushered Erica into the low-beamed room. A smudge of grey rushed past through their legs and into the dimly lit flag-stoned hall. It disappeared up the stairs.

'A Burmese?' asked Erica.

Vicky nodded. 'Ceremony will be off to lie on my bed in the sun.'

Their footsteps echoed across the boards as they walked between the islands of oriental rugs.

'Did you name the cat after Beltane?'

Vicky nodded. 'When she was a kitten, Rowan used to enjoy saying to visitors, do come in, please don't stand on Ceremony.'

Erica chuckled. 'Rowan's your partner...'

Vicky's expression changed. 'Passed on... ten years tomorrow.'

'I'm so sorry.' Slowly, as Erica's eyes adjusted to the shadows, more details became apparent. Everything looked timeless. Against a whitewashed wall, a grandfather clock slowly ticked. She stood in the connecting stone archway to the kitchen and looked around the dining room. Two canvases of abstract organic spiral forms hung on the wall.

Vicky busied herself with making the tea. 'Those are his paintings... he lived in a world of his own.' Her voice sounded distant.

Erica studied them. 'They're wonderfully mysterious...' Below on a sideboard sat a photograph of a young boy with pale blue eyes. Erica stooped to take a closer look, '...and this is your boy?'

'That's Will, or rather it was, ten years ago. Changed quite a bit now but he's still blond though. Will is into allsorts. He's very bright. Sam thought he would make a brilliant physicist one day, but he's gone off the rails a bit recently.'

Erica picked up the silver frame. She admired his strong features, and shock of hair. His face had something haunting about it. 'He must be a handsome lad now.'

'I see Rowan in him.' Vicky said, proudly.

'You've done so well to bring him up on your own.'

Vicky stood still for a moment, about to take the tray through into the small conservatory opening off the kitchen. 'Somehow, it would feel disloyal to start again. When my boy leaves, maybe… perhaps…' She left her thought hanging. 'Come on through.'

Erica stared out of the sunroom. The trees and undergrowth of the Oakenland lapped onto rough pasture like giant waves over a beach. Above them, the Hill rose up above the foliage like an island through a sea of deep green. 'It's gorgeous! You don't have a garden you have the whole landscape.' On the summit, through a thin shroud of mist, Erica could still make out the pale grey outline of the tall Hell Stone. She strained her eyes to detect any sign of life.

Vicky placed the cups on the coffee table and they settled themselves down on the loungers. 'So how are you feeling now, Erica?

'Perhaps it was the ride in the Morris but I feel like a teenager.' Erica sat back and sipped her tea. 'I had the feeling… like being on a high, when you're in tune with the universe and events take place in sequence, as though tied to each other like a string of beads. When things just happen naturally, as if everything is preordained, and occur without any effort.'

Vicky nodded. 'I know what you mean. Perhaps moving back to Dorset has triggered something within you?'

'It's obvious to me now, in London I became totally constrained by my surroundings,' Erica stated. 'Here, it's like that feeling after arriving in a foreign country, a sort of heightened awareness.' Erica paused. 'There's a problem though. Seeing everything in a new light is making me question things afresh…' Erica stopped; she knew what was playing on her mind; it was her marriage, but she did not want to talk about it to Vicky now, it was too soon in their friendship.

They looked out over the grassy slopes of the Hill, as the shadows of soft grey grew long, and the sky formed a backdrop washed with a cerise hue.

'I was going to ask you…' Erica threw Vicky a pleading look.

'Go on…' Vicky encouraged.

'…if you could tell me more about the festival. I had no luck with that woman in the library, what's her name, Beebee?'

Vicky looked understanding. 'She does get a touch protective over stuff I agree, but Bee's ok, when you get to know her. You just have to get on her side.'

'Hmm… well, bee or not, she's not exactly a hive of information, she wouldn't tell me a thing.'

'You have to appreciate she just believes it's bad luck to talk about the ceremony. So what do you want to know?'

'Whatever you can tell me.' Erica asked, eagerly, 'Miss Bird called it the Skimmity, isn't that different from Beltane?'

'In these parts, the early Church imposed their morality by trying to turn the pagan ceremony of Beltane into a shaming ritual called Skimmity. The name comes from the long wooden skimming spoon milkmaids used. The revellers used the spoons to beat the effigies of the people who'd been judged to have misbehaved. Kneebone still uses one as his drumstick.'

'Kneebone?'

'Mr Dodo Kneebone, our church warden… the drummer.'

'Ah, quite a little tyrant, I noticed he seemed to want to rule the roost.' Erica stopped herself; and wondered whether she had said the wrong thing.

Vicky continued. 'People just put up with him, I suppose, anyway, in World War II, the ceremony almost died out, with the young men away fighting, after all, the Horned One must be virile.'

Erica considered this for a second. 'I suppose celebrating Spring is all about fertility, isn't it? But I wouldn't have thought the vicar would be enthusiastic about that sort of thing.'

'Rodney takes an interest in everything,' Vicky said.

'Perhaps he feels guilty.'

'What for?' Vicky looked thrown.

'For what the church did in the past,' Erica explained. 'I can see they would want to throw the old beliefs into disrepute, so that the people would follow the new religion.'

'The Church suppressed all the old festivals,' Vicky explained. 'Yuletide became Christmas, and the Spring Equinox became Easter. In most places, they succeeded in substituting the Cross in place of the Maypole, but here tradition runs too deep.'

Erica gazed up to the Hell Stone megalith. 'If the Church and their henchmen were so intent on destroying everything, it's strange that so much has lasted from pagan times.'

'We've the local people to thank for preserving the stones and earthworks,' Vicky confirmed, 'and Beltane despite the Church. If you come to the service tomorrow,' Vicky suggested, 'you might find Rodney's sermon interesting, I think it's to be about Adam and Eve.'

'The truth is, Vicky,' Erica sighed, 'I just don't regard myself as a Christian.'

'Buddhist, Muslim, Hindu, Jew, Pagan - religion is like clothes. It's not what we wear Erica, but what we are underneath that counts.'

'Hmm…' Erica was doubtful. 'I wish I believed you.' She thought back to the suicide bomb headlines in the paper that morning.

'Rodney takes a broad view. In today's multi-cultural society, he has to draw people in, he needs to increase the attendances.'

Erica picked up some unease in Vicky's voice. 'The church is in danger of closing?' Erica enquired.

Vicky became troubled. 'He might be out of a job at any moment, or even worse moved to Birmingham.'

'That does sound a bit bleak, is he married?' Erica asked.

'His wife died, before he came here.' Her face stiffened. 'He's lived alone at the Manse with his housekeeper, Miss Tweedy, for over ten years now.'

'Ahh yes, the little woman standing next to Beebee on the bridge.'

'If you come to the service tomorrow,' Vicky sighed, 'you can make up your own mind about him.'

Erica removed her shawl. Vicky noticed Erica's necklace. 'That's unusual. May I look.'

Erica took off the narrow leather thong; attached to the end, a silver clasp held the small ammonite.

Vicky studied the fossil. There was a broken edge along one side. 'It must have meant something special for you to take the trouble to mount a broken fossil in a silver.'

'Just a keepsake from a happy episode in my life, a boy gave it to me as a birthday gift when I was fourteen.' Erica became reflective. 'I never knew his name and only met him once.'

Vicky looked pensive. 'On the bridge, your circlet of flowers was carried off in the arms of Awen and then it became hooked on that stick. That meant something. You may be married now, but... it was an omen.'

'Don't tell me...' Erica tried to make light of it. 'I'm going to meet a tall dark stranger,' she chuckled, 'with horns, no doubt.'

'Don't laugh,' Vicky did not alter her expression. 'I sense your ammonite and the omen on the bridge are, in some way, connected.'

'I can't see how the two incidents could be linked in any way, Vicky, they're over twenty-five years apart.' Erica stood up. She looked out at the Hill. The silhouette of the Hell Stone stood against the late afternoon sky. The pale silver orb of the full moon now shone. 'I didn't realise it was so late,' she said, brightly. 'Jet will be desperate for his walk. If I start back now I can still take him out before nightfall.'

'I'll drop you off.' Vicky fetched her car keys. 'Your husband will be wondering what's become of you.'

'I don't think so.' Erica failed to disguise her underlying sense of frustration. 'It's always me that's left wondering what Simon's up to.'

CHAPTER 6

The Brewery

To take advantage of sexual opportunity is a basic animal instinct of the predatory male.

Like a dog sniffing at the tail of a bitch on heat, the BMW followed the red Japanese soft-top along the country lanes towards Dorchester.

He inserted his favourite James Brown CD into the player. From the first rim shot on the snare, he was into the groove. 'Come on y'all… It's the soul patrol… Get down… I'm a sex machine…' He cranked up the volume to maximum and wound down all the windows. The steering wheel transformed itself into bongo drums. Disco dancing in his seat and shaking his body in time with the beat, he sped along the byways with the bass booming, like a boy racer.

Jazz funk is an acquired taste. He had picked up this partiality in his student days from too many late nights frequenting the Saint Louis Blues, a sweaty dive bar in Muswell Hill. Today, the music matched Simon's mood perfectly. Everything was going swimmingly and life was starting to fit his game plan. He had managed to capitalise on the chance encounter, and now the dice were falling in his favour.

'We have a win-win scenario,' he chuckled. 'Today's taking a turn for the better.'

As if he had been travelling in a time warp and transported back for the length of the journey, the end of the CD coincided neatly with his arrival behind Beth outside her apartment in the Victorian brewery. He squeezed his silver-grey coupé into the parking slot alongside her sports convertible. Briefly, he had lost thirty years and thirty pounds in weight, but then reality struck home. Beth stood over by the steps at the entrance and he was conscious of her watching him as his fifty-year old body became wedged in the narrow gap of the door opening against the side of her car. He wriggled free, his only option to allow his suit jacket to be pulled from his back. It fell in a crumpled heap across the front seat. With some difficulty, he retrieved it. While making squirming movements to the music still playing inside his head, he escaped from the constriction and swaggered across the yard over to Beth.

'No worries.' He slung the jacket over his shoulder.

Beth looked at him, quizzically. 'Cool,' she said and led the way through the shared entrance and up the steep steps. He began to spring up the stairs after her.

By the time Simon reached the first landing, Beth was already a flight ahead. She called back, 'Top level, I'm afraid.'

'Top level, cool.' Simon attempted to mirror her manner.

Beth bounded on, taking the steps two at a time. She reached the third floor, poked her head over the banister, and grinned down. 'The lift's not working.' Her voice echoed against the bare brick. 'Sorry.'

She had addressed him like an elderly grandparent and he needed to counter the insinuation. He strained his neck to look up. 'Keeps me fit.' He attempted to run up the remaining flight.

Beth gave him a sideways look and held open the door. 'Better get your breath back.'

'I think...' he panted like an aged bloodhound, 'I must be... a touch... out of form.'

She looked sympathetic. 'We'll have to see if we can't get you into condition.'

Simon intended to continue this beguiling line of chat once he had regained his breath but, when he entered her flat, he was awestruck. He had been half expecting a room not unlike his old student bed-sit, however when he crossed the threshold, he stepped into a page out of an Ikea catalogue. 'Great décor...' he gasped. 'I like the modern look.' He felt the need to make her aware of his being up with the latest mantra from the style gurus. 'Less is more...' he added.

She unlaced her Doc Martens and nodded. 'I keep things minimalist. More Zen than Mies.'

'Quite,' he said, and threw his crumpled jacket over the back of one of the glass dining chairs.

He was about to crash onto the cream, faux-leather sofa, when Beth demanded, 'Don't sit down.' For a second, he was taken aback.

'Trousers off...' she ordered, as if it were a command in a drill hall and his expression regressed to that of a bashful third-former, visiting the school nurse. 'We don't want marks on the furniture, do we?' This matronly tone produced instant compliance. Along with his shoes, he took off his trousers and meekly handed them over to her. Beth held both trousers and shoes out at arms length, and screwed up her nose. 'I'll give them a sponge down.' She began to walk away. 'Brazilian or Turkish?' she asked.

'Er...' For a second, Simon was lost. 'I think a Brazilian is more me, definitely.'

She looked over her shoulder and raised a critical eyebrow at him standing in his socks. 'Hmm...' She nodded. 'I prefer Calvin Klein myself.'

He glanced down at his crumpled, blue and white striped boxer shorts. That he would end up in a young woman's apartment in his underwear was the last thing he had planned when he had dressed that morning. However, in true public school spirit, he was determined to maintain an air of assured normality, regardless of what fate chose to throw at him.

Simon gazed about him at the room. It would have put an estate agent into hyphenated hyperbole overdrive with its double-height, bare-brick, timber-floored, open-plan, loft-living life-style. A huge abstract expressionist canvas took up most of one white wall. He had to raise his voice over the scrubbing noises and the gurgling coming from the galley kitchen. 'Did you do the place out yourself?'

'Nahh, turn-key project, my brother's in property.'

'Useful.' Simon wandered over to the bookcase.

Sensing that he had begun a tour of inspection, Beth shouted from the kitchen, 'Do have a shufti; you found the Malthus?'

'Thanks.' He carefully took down the edition of *Principles of Political Economy* with its battered leather binding and examined the frontispiece. 'Did you know Beth, both Darwin and Wallace came to the same conclusion on the survival of the fittest, after reading his *Essay on the Principle of Population?*'

'Yeh, amazin...' she replied from afar, 'how one idea can lead to another... init.'

Over coffee, they continued to talk at some length about Malthus. The light dawned on Simon - Beth was far from the run of the mill local newspaper reporter that he had assumed her to be. However, the more illumination cast, the more enticing became the prospect that lay ahead.

He had begun to wonder what the next step should be when Beth announced, 'You know, Malthus declared that all human actions are controlled by two primal urges, the need for food,' she paused, 'and the need for sex. What's more...' she continued, 'according to him, neither of those two urges can ever be satiated.'

Simon looked at her expectantly, as a dog might hang upon the next command of his mistress. 'Right, so... growled, 'you're telling me you're hungry.'

'Could be...' she said, with a mischievous grin.

'Fancy going out for a bite then?' he asked.

'Your trousers are still wet, why don't I ring for a pizza?' she suggested.

'Just the ticket.' Simon visibly became more excited by the prospect of the wider range of possibilities presented by the option of staying in.

Beth dialled and placed the order. 'Please do excuse me.' She sidled into the bedroom.

Simon took the chance to freshen up and wandered into the bathroom. Only when he glanced in the mirror did he realise just how ridiculous he looked. Being trouser-less might have put him at a psychological disadvantage, however he considered such an indignity well worth the price. After all, any state of undress was one step on the way to achieving intimacy, and he would be a fool to let such an opportunity pass him by. He must allow it to develop and reach its full potential, wherever that might lead. He beamed a self-satisfied congratulatory grin; it was no mean feat being able to talk in his underwear about Malthus, in the company of a twenty-three year old female journalist. That had to be one advantage of having reached a certain level of maturity; a younger man would have fallen at the first hurdle.

He removed his shirt and vest and splashed some water over his body. He shrugged his shoulders at the row of coloured bottles with French names on the glass shelf. Glancing at the label of the one that looked the least flamboyantly feminine, he unscrewed the top. 'What the hell,' he chuckled, and directed a perfunctory squirt at his groin.

He turned his profile to the mirror and held in his stomach, for a few seconds. On being forced to take a gulp of air, his stature returned to its former pufferfish-like state. He put his shirt back on without his vest and left the top three buttons undone, revealing the grey hairs on his chest.

Simon returned to the lounge. The other books on the shelves elicited raised eyebrows: *The Lovers' Guide to Politics*, *Machiavelli's Letters to his Daughter*, *The Marquis de Sade, A Biography*.

Simon took down *de Sade* and at random, he started to read… 'A poor fool indeed is he who adopts a manner of thinking for others.'

'Not me,' he scoffed. On hearing the bedroom door, he hurriedly replaced it back on the shelf.

He turned around and his jaw dropped. She was no longer the ginger-mopped butch kid. Now, she had let her hair fall over her neck in copper ringlets. This was more than a makeover - Beth had emerged from a camouflage cocoon and undergone a metamorphosis. Gone were the fatigues and army surplus. They were replaced by a loose-fitting, peacock blue, chiffon dress with low décolletage; it was cut on the bias and ended in points around her ankles. Her dress shimmered like the surface of a butterfly wing and she floated over to settle next to him, on the arm of the cream sofa.

Previously well hidden, a different woman was now unveiled - a shapely, sophisticated, seductive temptress with a deep enticing cleavage and an even more revealing back.

'Seen anything interesting?' she enquired.

Simon felt his heart race. He had the feeling that Beth might now be moving on from Malthus to other things less cerebral. He was aroused and, when he became aroused, he became intellectually incoherent. Simon fumbled for a handkerchief. He remembered it was in his trouser pocket. He smiled at her with as laid-back an expression as he could muster.

'You looking for tips?'

'Tips?' He was taken off guard.

Beth glanced across at the bookshelf. The Marquis de Sade lay askew.

'Ahh, just browsing.'

The doorbell chimed. 'Pizza!' a voice shouted.

'Let me get this,' Simon insisted and scurried over, stopping only to grab his wallet from his jacket pocket. Witnessing the transformation had caused Simon to forget his own state of dress.

He opened the door. The delivery boy gawped at Simon in his boxers. The spotty youth looked embarrassed as he announced, 'Large salami - hot and spicy.' He then added with a note of recognition, 'Hey, aren't you that political fella?'

Simon stared the lad in the eye and intoned in the manner of Obi-Wan Kenobi, 'You don't know me...' He handed over a twenty-pound note and added, 'Get my meaning...'

'Cheers, mate…' The boy pocketed the money and fell into a state of temporary hypnosis as he stared open mouthed over Simon's shoulder at the scene within.

Simon closed the door. When he turned around, Beth was caressing an olive-green bottle, covered in condensation.

'Chardonnay?' She rolled the word around her mouth as though her tongue were already caressing the wine within.

Two empty wine glasses sat on the coffee table, positioned with their bowls touching, provocatively.

Simon sauntered over in a deliberately casual manner and slid the pizza box across the surface.

She put out her hand to stop it shooting off the edge. 'Hold tight!' she commanded and thrust the bottle directly between his thighs.

He took in a sharp intake of breath.

Beth grasped the corkscrew, turned the tool around and pulled, vertically. The cold bottle slid up towards his groin and he gripped on to the neck with both hands. Beth began to rock in a reciprocating motion. Simon gave off the sound of a steam goods engine shunting up a steep incline, and his face turned red. The cork squeaked. Slowly, the stopper eased out of the neck.

Pop!

Their bodies collided and they grabbed hold of each other.

'Mmm you smell a bit nicer now.' She smiled. 'More cowslip than cowpat.'

It was their second full-on physical contact that day. More pleasant than when he had landed on the said offending article and Beth had fallen on top of him. They savoured the moment for a second, but then she began to laugh.

Simon joined in, and poured out the wine. 'Phew, that was an interesting bottle opening technique,' he chuckled, 'where did you learn that?'

'My gap year, I spent the summer in France with bottles of wine.'

Simon slurped the wine. 'What sorts are there?'

'All sorts: fluted, ones with high shoulders, sloping shoulders, or ones with wide shoulders and deep punts,' she continued.'

He glanced down at the base of her bare back. 'The dip in the bottom, you mean.' He smacked his lips. 'What a fascinating way to fill your gap.' Simon was exhilarated. Along with the change of dress, the press-girl had also undergone a change of personality. She had become a coquette and he found her captivating.

She nodded. 'All shapes and sizes; I've seen them all.'

Simon raised his eyebrows. 'I didn't realise there were so many.'

'I was under a very *au fait* vintner who gave me instruction in-depth.'

Simon hiccupped. 'So how many other ways are there to uncork a bottle?'

'Perhaps you'd prefer me to hold, and you to gyrate, next time?' Beth suggested. 'I'll put another one on ice for later.'

'I'm probably already over the limit...'

Beth's eyes flashed like a speed camera. 'Really...'

'There are already too many points on my licence...'

'Quite...' she said, knowingly.

'It was the front page of *the Echo* I was aiming for,' Simon scoffed, 'not the Sunday tabloids.'

'We do have your reputation to think about. We wouldn't want any scandal.'

'What about your wife,' Beth taunted, 'perhaps you should ring her.'

Simon was unruffled. He detected a hint of mock innocence in her voice. 'Well, I won't tell her if you don't. Damn! I just remembered, it's Erica's birthday tomorrow.'

'You'll just have to buy her something special.' She gave him an enquiring look.

'It's in the briefcase - we picked it up from the Green Man. It's a laptop.'

'Will the computer make up for you not keeping her warm tonight?'

'We don't share sleeping quarters any more.' Simon stated in a matter of fact tone.

'If you're a good boy, Simon, maybe I'll show you my laptop later?' she giggled and the diagonal overlap of her dress parted to reveal a shapely thigh.

'I'll brush my teeth,' he announced and headed for the bathroom. Beth's demure smile seemed to linger in his head. He had not planned to stay. The mission he had set himself earlier already accomplished, anything from that point fell under the heading of 'Any Other Business'.

Erica's birthday or not, tomorrow would take care of itself. Beth was everything that Erica was not, a temptation too great to resist. The makeover was not just visual. To Simon, Beth simply was no longer the same woman. In his present mood, he found the new raunchy Beth irresistible. In the space of one afternoon, a potentially tasty morsel had miraculously become an attractive delicacy. Now the transformation was complete, like any dish, he would enjoy what was on offer while it was hot.

By the time he returned, Beth had retired to the bedroom where the only light came from the goldfish tank, making contented gurgles in one corner. She was lying on the bed wearing nothing but a pair of skimpy burgundy silk briefs.

'Mmm... less is more,' chuffed Simon. Whatever he looked like in reality, in his mind he was now twenty years old. He smiled with a mischievous glint in his eye. The second bottle was on ice. He reached down and pulled it from the bucket. Iced-water dripped over the silk sheets. 'Let's see...' Simon drawled, trying to contain his all too obvious sense of excitement. He moved the bottle slowly towards her and then inserted it between her thighs.

'Jeeze...' she shrieked.

'Cool, no worries...' Simon's patter continued to mirror hers. He then knelt above her, took hold of the stopper in his teeth, and pulled.

'I'm holding on tight,' she giggled. 'I'm squeezing hard. Wow! I can feel it. Hey, you're rotating it from side to side.'

'Grrrrfffff.'

Pop!

'Wow, what a corker!' she squealed. Beth was getting tipsy.

The stopper had ended up in his mouth. The wine bubbled out onto her thighs.

'Oops,' Beth feigned concern, 'a touch more punch than I thought…'

'Yefff… quite,' Simon burbled. He fingered his teeth to judge whether they were intact before casually casting the cork over his shoulder. It made a satisfying 'plop' in the goldfish tank. He swaggered, with an inane grin, and started to lick up the surplus.

Beth chuckled, 'Mr Janus, you've certainly got bottle.'

'S'pose I *am* a bit of a vintage,' Simon growled, smugly. 'Now, just what did you learn in your gap year?'

CHAPTER 7

The Find

'SIMON'S NOT HOME… TYPICAL.' Erica walked through the gate, and waved back as Vicky drove off in the Morris. Jet was waiting on the mat. He bounded up. 'I know… it's been a long time since breakfast.' She had become lost in conversation with Vicky, and now guilt beset her at having left the dog alone all day. There was only one way to make amends, a brisk walk up the Hill, before dark fell.

The dog followed her upstairs, and she put the brooch on Sarah's bedside table. She noted the spot of dried blood, which marked the point where the pin had pricked her finger. Her head buzzed with the events of the last few hours. The walk would give her a chance to settle her mind after her day at the ceremony and meeting Vicky.

'Come on, then,' she sighed, 'my bath will just have to wait.' She took the dog-lead and small torch from the drawer in the hall table and, within a few minutes, they were out on the muddy path up through the woods.

The dog ran on, and they began the climb. Jet was exceptionally frisky. She tried to keep up with him, but the evening mist made the path slippery. The cool moist air felt electric, and acted like an agent on her mind, working its magic, to invigorate, clarify and distil her thoughts.

She caught sight of a faint glimmer of flames in the distance and felt a vague sense of unease. Jet was acting strangely. Every few minutes, he stopped dead, cocked his head and raised an ear. He dodged this way and that, and charged into the undergrowth like a ground-hugging missile. At times, he became lost in the shadows of the bushes and trees. He seemed to pick up a sense of excitement at abnormal activity, and made whiny barks.

She had often thought he had sixth sense. It brought to mind her library book about psychic pets - the book had even related how dogs for epileptics had the ability to give their owners warning of the onset of a fit, before they would be aware of it themselves.

Like a student in the exam room, traditional science left the difficult questions alone... only where the topic was well understood, could it provide answers.

rronk rronk rronk

The noise diverted Erica from her thoughts. The source increased in volume. A skein of Brent Geese flew over directly above. They were coming up from the south coast where they would have wintered in the wetlands. She squinted toward the setting sun and followed their flight. Against the wispy thin cerise cloud of the evening sky, their configuration hardly altered as they traced a line toward the top of the Hill.

In an instant, the noise changed pitch. As though they had picked up a signal by radio control, the formation altered direction. Soon, they were distant specks out over the wide horizon to the northwest, heading for summer breeding grounds in the Arctic.

Perhaps their inbuilt direction-finders had been triggered by a change in the earth's magnetism over the Hill? How could such abilities transfer from one generation to the next? Perhaps at one stage, such talents were available to humans too, but now, only the gifted few practiced them. Do we not have a responsibility to build on whatever gift we possess, for the benefit not only of the individual but also for the gene pool of succeeding generations?

Jet had strayed far on ahead. She stood still, in order to catch any sign of movement and strained her eyes in the fading light. Far up on the top of the Hill, she could still discern the flicker of the flames.

There was no sign of her dog. A sense of disquiet descended. She called his name and listened intently for a response. As she continued to climb along the spiral path, she searched for any sign until she reached the Ladypool.

Even in daylight, the pool was a strange place, but in the dim twilight, it became yet more mysterious. The reflection of the thinly veiled moon floated in the dark water.

One by one, the stars became visible. To the north, the ruins of St Catherine's chapel formed an eerie silhouette in the fading grey. Behind the pool to the south, cast in darkness, the land rose sharply, creating a steep rocky outcrop.

She was about to turn around, when from above came the rattle of falling stones. She shone her torch toward the noise. The fading beam tracked from side to side. In places, the surface of the rock glistened.

The climb up behind the pool was difficult. Several times, she lost her footing and slipped on the dank moss. She pulled herself up onto the rock ledge, and stood still to listen. At first, there was no sight or sound. Then, in the torchlight, on the flat rock, next to the ferns, something reflected… paw prints. Brushing apart the wet ferns, she bent down and pushed her way through the foliage on her hands and knees.

'Jet, where are you?' A whine answered her. She put her hand forward in the darkness and her fingers touched something warm. It was his backside. He was shivering. 'Come on, boy…' she coaxed. Slowly, he emerged backwards from the shadows, his tail held taut between his legs. 'Silly… getting jammed in there…'

Eventually, he was out, and he lay down on his front legs, panting. 'What's wrong?' She put out her hand and stroked him, and recognised he was trembling not with fear, but with excitement.

A hard rattle rang out. Whatever he had been holding had dropped onto the rock between his front paws. The dog edged back over it. 'What have you found?'

She shone her torch and the object sparkled. She crouched down and cautiously picked it up. Instinctively, she held it high against the moon. 'How wonderful…' she whispered. The pale orb of the moon fragmented into shards of blue and yellow, breaking into a thousand light splinters to form a myriad of miniature iridescent rainbows. '… A crystal.'

As wide as her palm, she cupped it in one hand and shone the dimming torchlight onto the find. Its form entranced her. She knew that quartz naturally fashioned itself into prism shapes, but she had never before seen anything natural with such faultless geometry… a perfect pyramid with four triangular sides. She held it up to study it.

The more she looked, the more astonishing the stone became. She rotated it between her fingers… so many surfaces unfolded. A pale reflection of the moon appeared on a thin fault-line across the centre of the prism. It acted like a projection screen. It mesmerized her. She fell into a trance.

Flame of light, flame of love… flame of life

Kindle our spirit from the spark of the stars.

Kindle our souls from the light of Maia's glory…

CHAPTER 8
The Visitation

'NOW WHERE'VE YOU GONE?' The dog had disappeared again. Erica shone the torch onto the rock shelf to see if she could detect any new paw prints. As she did so, the beam dimmed.

'Damn battery...'

A cloud covered the moon. She struggled to make out anything other than the outline of the rocks against the night sky. She scrambled back down the cliff face and eventually, after slipping over and grazing her knee, she found herself back at the edge of the pool. It took several minutes of looking and listening before she convinced herself that he must have headed home on his own. In no mood to continue up the Hill, she turned her back on the distant flames.

Only the occasional brief interlude of moonlight guided her steps down through the wood. Every few yards she stopped to call out, 'Come on boy! Where are you?' but there was no response. Then, after stumbling down a slope she heard a rustle in the undergrowth. Something moved. She strained her eyes, was someone in the shadows? She stopped calling out.

She reached the bottom and half ran up to the gate, hoping Jet would be there. Her heart sank - there was no sign of him.

On the step, something else was waiting for her. It glistened under the porch-light. A small cylindrical package wrapped in dull gold. There was no note. It could not be for Sarah, her friends would know she was away in Dorchester. She unwrapped it, it was a bottle bath essence. She took the gift upstairs and put the bottle to her nose. 'Perhaps it's from Vicky? That was nice of her.'

She would just have to wait for Jet to return on his own. There was no point going out again. He would turn up eventually. The pets described in her book travelled hundreds of miles back to their owners. She opened the bedroom window in order to hear his bark should he arrive. Erica looked out again. Nothing stirred. Why had he run off? Perhaps Jet had felt pulled by the activity on the Hill. Erica stared again out into the blackness.

Jet was not the only one missing. Where was Simon? The last time she had seen him was outside the pub with that journalist. 'I wonder which stray is going to turn up first...' In Simon's study, she phoned his mobile and left a message. She took the crystal from her coat pocket and placed it next to the computer.

Erica gazed out blankly through the dark glass. The clouds covered the moon. Her reflection stared back at her from the blackness. Then, gradually, the image changed. The countenance of a younger woman became evident - a beautiful face with long blonde hair and adorned by flowers.

She closed her eyes. A few seconds later, she opened them to find her own reflection once more. She raised her hands to her head - the crown was gone. Who was girl? What was happening?

Erica began to panic. Was she losing her wits? She needed to find something to occupy her. It was still only nine o'clock. She switched on Simon's computer. After making a few musical beeps, it logged itself onto the net. She spelt out a name in the search window, 'Osser'. It came up with only one result.

'Canon Charles Herbert in Somerset and Dorset Notes and Queries in 1891 described the mask as cut from a solid block, excepting the lower jaw, which is movable, and connected with the upper by a pair of leathern hinges. A string, attached to this movable jaw, passes through a hole, and is then allowed to fall into the cavity.'

'It says nothing about the origins.' She noticed a footnote. 'It is said to be associated with Cernunnos.' She thought back to her lessons in the history of art. She could still remember some of the lectures on mythology. Her memory had never provided her with the ability other than to achieve average in her examinations but, for crossword puzzles and pub quizzes, it did the job quite capably. Her mind was often a disorganised jumble, but she did have an ability to dip into her subconscious and access half-remembered facts and to make intuitive connections.

She knew the Celts had many pagan gods, and their deities represented various combinations of human and animal forms. On hearing the word, Cernunnos, an image of a beautifully decorated Celtic cauldron had come into her mind. What was it called… she tried to remember… the Gunde… something? She thought hard… then typed into the search engine 'Gundes Cauldron'.

Within a couple of seconds, it responded… 'Gundestrup Cauldron?'

'That's the one…' she exclaimed in satisfaction and read out the text. 'The interior relief of the Gundestrup Cauldron, a 1st-century BC vessel, provides a striking depiction of the horned Cernunnos as Lord of the Animals, seated in the lotus position and accompanied by a ram-headed serpent; in this role he closely resembles the Hindu god Shiva in the guise of Pashupati, Lord of Beasts.'

Shiva… How could the worship of the same icon span such great distances? The image on the screen showed a snake in one hand, and the torc in the other. Did it mean that the origin of the Horned One was older than both Celtic and Indian civilizations? Perhaps they both shared a common ancestry.

Erica picked up the crystal and returned upstairs to prepare for her bath, the image of the snake and the ring still in her mind. She looked into the tall mirror and considered her figure - her hair a natural auburn, still without a trace of grey. Why did Simon no longer find her attractive? Perhaps her breasts were not as pert and her waist not as slender, but at forty, she was at ease with her body, and she felt womanly.

The prospect of her bath was now even more welcome. She lit three candles in a row next to the taps, and placed the crystal next to the candles.

She removed the gold paper from the gift. Inside was a small bottle of orange coloured liquid. No writing was on the label only a strange symbol, a square diamond divided into four triangles by a cross. The sign looked ancient and mysterious. Unscrewing the lid, the seal broke and Erica held the bottle to her nose. It must be bath oil. It smelt wonderful. She tried to decipher the mixture of aromas… lemon… mint… and underlying these, mustier earthy smells, like walking in the Oakenland after an April shower.

Gradually, she tipped the orange liquid into the bath water. Momentarily, she became mesmerised. The room filled with an intoxicating fragrance and before she knew it, the bottle was empty.

She lowered herself into the water. The foam caressed her body as though she were covered by the lightest of feather eiderdowns. Reflections from the candle flames mirrored on the surface of every bubble to create dancing patterns across the soapy suds. She relaxed and let the essence soak into her as the heady scent rose up in the steam. Erica took in deep breaths and a feeling of serene pleasure took over. The vapours opened up the pores in her skin, and filtered through channels in her mind allowing thoughts and images to flood her senses.

She stared into the crystal. Its geometry was flawless yet the minor surface imperfections gave the feel of it being completely natural. 'It's amazing…' The inclusion became more evident. It met the sides of the prism and formed a perfect square, creating an inner surface. She held it to the window. As she revolved it, at a certain angle, the faint image of the moon lay captured within.

Other than the fault line across the centre, there seemed no other impurities. A blue tint gave it an eerie luminescence that seemed to amplify the ambient light. Fossils, crystals and precious stones had always held a fascination, but this was special. Enthralled by its shape and colour she whispered the words again, 'It's amazing, so pure…' She closed her eyes and took long, slow, deep breaths from the rising vapours. An image appeared - unmistakable red eyes - the face of the Horned

Beast, a torc... two fires...a wooden throne... a moving light in the sky... a prayer came to her...

Truth in our hearts, strength in our hands

Vision in our eyes and purpose in our minds

May the power of love bring life to our souls

The image melted away. The fragrance filled her senses. She gazed through the steam at the candlelight - a ghostly white silhouette appeared - an ancient outline cut into the chalk hill. She knew the figure only a few miles from Witchbury... the Cerne Giant.

She lay, staring until...

Click.

Her dreams were brought to an abrupt halt. Was it the door latch? She grabbed her dressing gown and ran to the top of the stairs. She turned on the light.

Ping! The bulb had blown... darkness.

CHAPTER 9

The Dream

ERICA STOOD STILL AND half whispered, 'Simon...'

It was just another noise - the wind against the letterbox, the boiler igniting, the plumbing groaning. She put on her sandals and tried to tiptoe down the stairs, but her footsteps were uncertain, each step on the old oak boards echoed, every squeak became amplified in the shadows. She edged into the darkness, and her fingers crept along the wall as she felt for the hall light-switch.

Click...

Briefly, the brightness dazzled. The first thing that came into view was the hall cupboard door... it had swung open.

She dashed downstairs. Outside in the lane, she looked up and down but saw no-one. An owl hooted. The cool of the night calmed the heat of her body under her gown. It was the last night of April. The moon shone clear against the sky, full of stars. She glanced at the Seven Sisters. One star shone unusually bright.

Erica felt intoxicated and returned to the hall. She shook her head in disbelief at the sight of the coats and blankets in disarray in the cupboard. She would tidy them in the morning. Climbing the stair, she had to grab hold of the rail. She staggered to the bathroom to collect the crystal. Back in her room, Erica threw herself on top of the bed. Light from the digital clock reflected into the blue interior of the crystal. She stared into it and lost herself inside the kaleidoscope of fractal light.

The bath oil had been absorbed into her skin and as she lay on the duvet, the rich fragrance enveloped her. She closed her eyes, spinning with a whirlpool of images from the day.

A gorilla with a clerical collar stood in the pulpit, frothing at the mouth, and holding up one fist and hitting the Bible with the other. 'Thou shall have no other god but me.' She looked down at herself, covered in thick brown fur. The Silverback bellowed; in response, the congregation of female gorillas bayed and bawled. Then, the congregation disappeared. She had heard a single plaintive bark...

The full moon lit the way through the trees. Shadows played across the path up the Hill. Some distance ahead, a presence moved - she followed the dark shadow and let it guide her. She glided along the earth path, up through the woods and past the reflected moon captured in the dark circle of the Ladypool. The path spiralled anti-clockwise up the Hill. How long it took to reach the grassed embankment of the ancient Cursus, she had no idea but, when she arrived at the summit she felt invigorated, and viewed the scene before her, as though she were invisible in the darkness.

The Hell Stone and the Altar were awash with silver shadows. The silhouette of the giant monolith stood stark and black against the pale orange-grey to the northeast, about to herald the dawn of a new day. The embers of two large fires glowed yellow on both sides of the Altar. Occasional sparks shot up into the night sky and illuminated a wooden throne.

Something moved. Against the moonlit sky, figures rose up. Slowly, the group formed a wide circle encompassing the fires. Five female figures, dressed in long white gowns, glided around a tall masculine outline. The profile of his muscular torso glowed scarlet in the afterglow. The embers bathed his skin with a red radiance.

The mask evident in the light of the flickering flames was familiar... the beard, the hair, the horns.

'You've come…' The voice echoed over the heath. He turned to beckon a sixth female. The newcomer drew closer. The girl was guided to take her place upon the throne; her golden hair glistened in the moonlight.

The two figures echoed the stone forms - he the megalith, she the Altar. Now, in his left hand, Erica caught the spark of a curved mirrored surface - a silver torc. In his right hand, he held her crown of flowers. He crowned her with the circlet of May blossom and placed the torc around her neck.

'I am the sun,' he proclaimed.

'I am the moon,' she responded.

'I am heaven,' he breathed.

'I am earth,' came her whispered reply.

'I am hard, as the Anvil of Cern',

'I am soft as the water of the Awen.'

He lowered himself down to kneel before her. Taking her hands in his, he placed them on the horns. The girl gripped each one tightly. The heavy mask lifted with ease, as though the girl had the strength of two men. She placed it on the ground between the two fires.

The girl looked upon the face kneeling in front of her. Long blond hair flowed over his ears and neck. Slowly, he raised his head toward her. 'Wyllow!' the girl exclaimed.

'I am hot as the Beltane fire!' he cried, and he took a burning log from the fire. His eyes stared and sparkled as he held the stick high. 'Let this fire burn out evil and illuminate the just.' He dragged the flame up and down over his body.

The log broke in two. The pieces crashed into the cinders. The embers came alive. Threads shot up and danced into the night sky, and wove a tapestry of red, amber and gold.

He reached out and took the girl by the hands. The two entwined between the fires, crossing each other's path.

The others began to clap in time as the momentum of the beat grew. First, they gathered around as the two moved closer together. Then, they danced - shouting and whooping with abandon.

After a while, the clapping slowed. They gasped excitedly for breath. The two turned to face each other. He held something in his hands and offered it to the girl. 'Hail Priestess of Light,' he proclaimed. 'The chosen one…' He smiled as he pinned the bronze spirals upon her breast.

'I Sarah… I Sarah… I Sarah…' she chanted.

****

Three thousand miles away to the west, the sun was setting. The pattern of the heavens had now become visible against the darkening sky. On the balcony of his apartment, Dr Christopher Credus looked through a telescope to the north of Orion toward the extremity of Taurus, and found the Pleiades.

'I see you're on the prowl again, Doc.' His neighbour shouted over to him and chuckled.

'I've found a beauty, Mrs B! She has the face of a Botticelli painting. You wouldn't believe how stunning she is. A goddess, with six sisters who dance around her and tonight they wear robes of fire.'

'So what does your star goddess tell you?'

'To embark upon a journey, a call as strong as the force that connects the sun with the moon.'

'You'd better get your bags packed then, Doc, and follow your star.'

CHAPTER 10

The Meditation

TRUTH IS ONLY EVIDENT by our perception. The ebb and flow of the tide of waking tosses bizarre flotsam onto the shoreline of consciousness. In an instant, the veil of time covers all, and can cause us to be no surer of the memories of real events than fading images of things imagined.

Erica woke with the ghosts of the night inhabiting her thoughts. She whispered her daughter's name, hoping to slow the images fading - a group of figures in amber cloaks gathered around two fires.

A voice intruded and a different truth imposed itself. 'What is now proved was once only imagined...'

Erica jumped.

'...listen to Radio 4, tonight at 9pm - In our Time, with Melvyn Bragg...' The Greenwich time pips, told her she was awake and the green digits on the clock radio changed to 07:00. 'It's Sunday, the first of May. This is Charlotte Green. Good morning, here is the news....'

She hit the snooze button. Rays from the morning sun poured in through the open window and struck the crystal. She stared at the refracted rainbows shimmering above her on the ceiling. A chorus of birdsong assaulted her ears.

She turned to look out across to the Hill. Nothing seemed out of place. Did she expect the landscape to have faded like her dreams?

A realisation struck her - for the first time in twenty years, she had woken on her birthday without another soul in the same house. Sarah was at Liz's, and Simon was still astray. Perhaps it was all for the best, she needed the space to come to terms with the night and was thankful to have the house to herself. She put on the towelling robe and made her way to the bathroom.

On the landing, she came to a standstill, and looked at the carpet. A trail of dried mud led down the stairs. She felt a cool draught flow against her skin and her heart began to race in alarm. She hurried down to the hallway to find the front door wide open.

She stared at the scene outside to try to make sense of whatever clues she could find. Alongside footprints on the path, lay muddy paw marks. She called out from the threshold - 'Jet…' and ran to the gate. She looked up and down the lane… nothing.

Her mind filled with questions. Hope and disquiet surged through her in equal measure - something had happened in the night, but what? She needed to talk.

On the phone, the voice responded with a stifled yawn, followed shortly by a cheery chant. 'Happy birthday Erica…'

'Thanks for reminding me.' Erica's tone sounded more cynical than she had intended.

Vicky guessed that something was wrong. 'What's up?'

'Jet's disappeared - last night, on the Hill.'

'So you went up there after all?' Vicky asked, warily.

'Just as far as the pool, we never made it to the top.'

'I'm sure he'll find his way back sooner or later. Come to the service this morning,' Vicky suggested, 'and I'll help you look for Jet afterwards?'

Erica gave in. 'You know it's not really me but…'

Vicky brightened. 'I'll come over to pick you up at ten.'

Erica brooded. In Sarah's room, amongst the other family snaps on the pin-board, her fingers strayed to touch the photo of her daughter. Could mothers and daughters share thoughts? Last night was a dream, but her heart told her she had witnessed something real. She had always tried to give Sarah the space to allow her own personality to blossom, but she worried too. She knew Sarah had secrets. She looked at Sarah's bedside table. Something was missing. Where was the brooch? She was so sure she had left it there. She searched under the pillow and under the bed, but there was no sign of it. What would Sarah say? Erica felt deflated. Last night, had she unknowingly picked it up? Dejected, she returned downstairs to tidy the coats' cupboard.

In Simon's study, she put on Vivaldi's Four Seasons. For the first time since her student days, she felt the need to meditate. She sat down crossed-legged in the middle of the floor and stared at her painting. The two five-letter words were spaced out in red and grey letters across the large canvas. Each letter of the word CHAOS painted in red had the corresponding letter from the word ORDER painted in grey below it.

It was the end of term at St Martin's - the final year show. Simon had bought her painting. He had asked to meet the artist and they were introduced - she had delivered the painting to his flat. He had invited her out. They went for a meal. They had returned to his flat for the night. He had said it reminded him of a word-game. She remembered him remarking that people also can transform over time just like the game, step by step.

Is that what happened, had she changed like the word?

She closed her eyes, took slow deep breaths and a chant replayed in her mind - I Sarah… I Sarah… I Sarah… Her breathing echoed the rhythm of her heart, and soon she slipped into another realm…Her mind flipped over as she repeated the mantra.

There is a blank and then in front of her a stone wall appears. An old wooden gate with metal studs and with an ancient key hanging on the wall beckons to her - she unlocks it and enters. Revealed within is a beautiful garden, a robin sings. In the centre, a white spiral staircase leads up into the blue sky.

She does not recognise the garden but as she begins to climb the stair, her viewpoint starts to change. The scene is the Oakenland and the Hill. She ascends high above until she is able to look down over the whole landscape, which stretches out before her like pieces of a giant jigsaw puzzle.

Two paths twist up around the Hill, they form a double spiral. At the summit, they transform into two lazy wisps of smoke, which rise from the embers of two fires into the still air. Two snakes entwine into the spirals of a double helix. The form rotates in front of her. It becomes the interlock on Sarah's brooch.

The Hell Stone and the Altar crown the Hill. The precipice looks over Devil's Drop into the hidden valley to the church where the Portal Stone lies at the centre of in Cauldron Field. Half way up the Hill is the Ladypool - a circle of darkness. She stares intently into its depths and in doing so it takes on the form of a scrying mirror of obsidian. Reflected within appears a woman dressed in white with long golden hair...

Flora stirs upon white sheets

turns to tell that winter's gone

She rises with the crocus, writes not with words

but with the sound of bees

In perfumed fragrances she dances

amid confetti torn from the trees

She flirts and hides from view

and plays amongst the woodwind reeds.

She paints her masterpiece anew

- a pastel palette of chalk pinks and fine greens

She tells the world - 'summer's yet to come.'

Then sleeps and dreams.

CHAPTER 11

The Sermon

'IT'S MY FAULT WE'RE late, I lost track of time.' Erica stared at the tower ahead.

'Don't worry.' Vicky turned the Morris at Hobbs Cross toward the church. St Michael's stood next to Cauldron Field - composed, serene and isolated. It remained a testament to the faith of the original builders - spared, until now, from the vicissitudes of history.

As they approached, Erica gazed through the car window and noticed the state of the roof with its dislodged slates. 'It's strange,' she continued, 'to think that when the church was being built, the Oakenland was already ancient.'

Vicky parked and led the way up to the porch. 'Rodney says it may have supplanted a holy place more than twice as old again.'

Erica heard the sound of the organ and felt uneasy. 'We're late now we'll have to contend with black looks.'

Vicky was untroubled. 'Rodney's not the ogre you make him out to be,' she whispered, and pushed the dark oak door. It swung open and it squeaked, loudly.

'I wasn't thinking about Rodney,' Erica replied, 'but about his entourage.'

'Shhh…' Vicky lifted her finger to her lips.

They ventured in. It took time for Erica to become accustomed to the dim light. She failed see the old tin bucket half way up the aisle. The crash echoed around, for what seemed an eternity. The music stopped. The ladies on the front row looked around.

'It's there for the drips.' Vicky whispered. She waved a perfunctory acknowledgement toward the front row. The ladies had arranged themselves in order of size. Like bookends, Bunty Bagwash sat on the left, while on the far right sat Miss Tweedy.

Red-faced, and steered by Vicky, Erica fell onto the nearest empty pew and looked about her. The church was about a third full. The choir filed in, and took their positions. Erica recognised some of them as cleaned up versions of the village lads who had been chiding the procession with sticks. One in particular, a ginger-haired freckle-faced boy, about ten-years-old, stood out. He had looked so unholy yesterday, but now appeared the picture of innocence. A florid fanfare drew her attention to the organ enclosure. A bulbous nose and bearded chin, peered out at her.

A cascading riot of key changes heralded Rodney Radpole at the pulpit. After more crescendos, the Reverend began. 'Let us pray.'

Vicky nodded toward her hassock – the cover had a Burmese cat embroidered upon it. She placed it on the floor and knelt. Erica noted the snake on her own prayer cushion and remained seated.

Radpole addressed the congregation in a slow, affected ecclesiastical tone. 'Seek that which is flowering and unfolding within you. Find that which ignites your fire. Bless us with growth and abundance.'

'Amen', the congregation echoed.

'Let us spend a few moments in silent contemplation as we align ourselves with the Holy Spirit.'

Erica felt uncomfortable. The cream robes with elaborate gold embroidery gave her the feeling she was attending a medieval ritual.

The Reverend Radpole looked in Erica's direction. 'It's good to see some new faces amongst us. Heads once more turned. 'Let us begin with number twenty-three in your hymnbooks - All Things Bright and Beautiful.' The organ struck up with a flourish and the congregation sang.

They reached the end. The Reverend bowed, peered over his glasses toward the congregation, and, in measured tones, began a sermon. 'May is a time of arcane lore; a strange and curious time rich with possibilities. A time to celebrate, a time to rejoice in Eros and awaken him from his slumbers, a time of fecundity and of love.'

A slow, shuffled undulation travelled along the front pew, and ended with a squeak under Miss Tweedy.

The Reverend gathered pace. 'May is a time to celebrate the joy of youth - fire, energy, and light - a time to allow ourselves to grow and reach our true potential - a time to allow our spirits to unfold, to blossom, to dance.'

Erica wondered if Beebee had ever let herself unfold, blossom and dance.

'Let us consider our own mythical monster. This otherworldly beast is driven through the streets and fields, capering, cavorting and pulsating to the rhythm of drums. It celebrates procreation. Neither male nor female can function alone without the other. The sun, impregnates the earth with its seed, then new life begins.'

More minor tremors quaked the front pew.

'This weekend, as it has been for many thousands of years, our village is bedecked in ribbons of red and white.'

Erica decided Radpole was trying to do what the clergy had done before him - to usurp the power of the pagan for the benefit of the Church. Her mind began to wander and she fell into a daze… and gazed at the mosaic of stained glass. It depicted a shooting star, gold against an azure sky. His words were lost until she resurfaced at the mention of the word spring.

'What is it? It's a helix that represents the continuity of life - a double spiral the code of life itself. A spring is also a source of water - the elixir of life, as in our own Ladypool. And what of the word May?'

Erica was now fully alert.

'Where do we get the word? Some say it comes from the mother of Buddha - Maya. Coincidentally, Buddha's first symbolic act was to accept a dish of curds from a maiden on the first full moon of May, the greatest of Buddhist festivals. The drumstick used in the Skimmity, a milkmaid's skimming spoon separates the curds from the whey.'

Erica was intrigued - a tableau of a cow jumping over the moon and Little Miss Muffet came into her head.

He glanced over to the organ mirror, whereupon a hand held up the giant wooden spoon. The Reverend continued. 'Although we do not believe the festival is linked with Buddha, who can tell? In some ways, perhaps the pre-Christian world was smaller than it is today. I will now call upon Beebee to lead the congregation with her prayer, who tells me she composed this especially for today.' He directed a broad smile down at the front row.

In her yellow top and black skirt, a self-conscious Beebee ascended the creaky pulpit steps and read out her prayer in a practiced voice.

'Mother spirit of the Earth, connect us with thy sensuality

Let us celebrate the act of union between man and woman, between God and Goddess

Let us celebrate this time of joining, relating, and harmonizing energy

Let us become whole through the union of male and female.'

Beebee smiled and nervously returned to her place. The ageing woodwork groaned. A mild look of surprise greeted her from the ladies on the front row.

Radpole returned to his reading. 'And God said, let there be light, and there was light.' A beam from the sun burst through the stained glass. The ladies gazed at Erica. Showered in yellow and orange, and set aflame with colour, she felt as though she were on stage.

Radpole continued. 'Although in paradise, Adam felt alone in the Garden of Eden and so he asked God for a mate. God caused a deep sleep to fall upon Adam, and took one of his ribs and made woman.'

'He's talking as though it actually happened,' Erica thought. 'He can't expect us to believe in this?'

Radpole peered over the top of his glasses. 'They were both naked and were not ashamed.' He paused. 'Adam fell in love with Eve. She took advantage of that trust. By eating the forbidden fruit given to him by Eve, we forever must endure mortality, guilt and shame in nakedness. Satan, tricked Eve into tasting the forbidden fruit. She committed the original sin, and caused man's exile from Paradise. The Reverend continued, 'As any father would, God punished them both for their disobedience.'

'Blame it on the woman,' Erica thought, 'He is so patronising.' She suppressed an urge to stand up to state the case for the defence. She gave Vicky a look, pointed to the hassock and mouthed, 'It was the snake's fault.' Erica's whisper emerged louder than she intended.

Radpole stared at Erica with the air of a prosecuting barrister. She challenged his look.

Radpole concluded with the Lord's Prayer, and images of the Garden of Eden came to Erica. Eventually, the change of pitch in the drone of the Reverend's voice signalled the service was drawing to a close. 'In 1644, our ecclesiastical ancestors deemed fit to pass a law to banish all Maypoles from England. I'm glad to say, our parish is still in defiance of that law. I hope no one will be burnt at the stake as a result today.'

Subdued chuckles rippled around the church.

'I would remind you we need to raise one hundred thousand pounds for St Michael's roof. Thanks to the Ladies' Circle who raised thirty-seven pounds fifty at last week's bring-and-buy sale.' His eyes alighted once more on the front pew. 'My sincere thanks of appreciation...' he smiled ingratiatingly. The grand total, to date, stands at five thousand and three pounds, fifty pence. However, I hope to have some news soon, which may help keep the wolf from our door.' Against the fanfare from the organ and led by the ginger freckled lad, the choirboys filed out.

The congregation gathered themselves in groups and moved toward the lobby. The Ladies' Circle talked animatedly amongst themselves as they paraded down the aisle. Bunty Bagwash brought up the rear, her face the colour of beetroot.

Vicky mouthed the words 'won't be long', and headed for the vestry.

Erica waited until the church emptied. She then walked slowly toward the lighted candles in the chancel. Something pulled her past the wooden altar screen and she sat down in the heavy oak stalls where the ginger choirboy had been sitting.

The stone arch at the junction of the chancel and the transept terminated with a gargoyle. It spoke to Erica of distant times, of a heritage pre-dating Christianity. The face, part beast, part human, stared down. She turned towards the side window. Who were they? They looked like miners, with their leather skullcaps. She turned to the east window - a woman dressed in white. She caught her breath. The figure was beautiful, timeless. The gothic script announced her as St Catherine, and to the left was a wheel. In the bottom right hand corner, she noticed a small cross within a square diamond.

Erica felt a power rise through her. From the very place under her feet, it connected her to the cosmos. Her hand came to rest on the end of the bench and she found herself touching something round and smooth. It felt soft, warm and comforting. For a few seconds she dared not look down.

****

Simon leapt down the staircase of the Old Brewery with a spring in his step and a beam on his face. Sunday morning, the sun shone and everything was right with the world - well, almost everything. He had left his mobile phone in the BMW and it was not until he squeezed back in, and listened to Erica's message about their missing dog, that her birthday resurfaced in his mind - still, he had bought her the computer.

He turned on the ignition. The CD began to play from where it had ended the previous afternoon. As though nothing of any significance had happened in the interim eighteen hours, Simon took up from the same point. 'Come on y'all… It's the soul patrol… I'm a sex machine… Get down…' Nothing had happened, other than he had spent the night with an attractive, twenty-three year-old woman.

CHAPTER 12

The Search

ERICA WHISPERED, 'IT WAS Jet... I was stroking Jet.'

Vicky had returned from the vestry to discover Erica on the end of the choir stall, caressing a carved oak head of a beast.

Erica looked shaken. Her eyes were moist.

Vicky tried to help her to stand. 'You're missing your dog, don't worry, he'll turn-up.' Vicky picked up a shopping basket, and took Erica by the arm. 'Come on', she said with a brisk tone, 'we'll look for him.'

They started off, towards the porch, but Erica hesitated. 'This might sound silly but I'm not sure I feel up to an encounter with the Reverend, just now.'

Vicky nodded toward the side door. 'We'll go that way.'

They circled the rear of the church and walked under the tower. A blue rope tied to a brass hook at the base of the tower wall caught Erica's attention. Above, it disappeared through a hole warn by age in the black timber of the mezzanine platform.

Vicky noticed Erica's puzzled look. 'That's the Tenor Bell... it's rung when there's something important - a celebration or a warning - that's Dodo Kneebone's job. He's verger, and organist too,' Vicky said.

'Quite a Quasimodo…' A low, emissive groan caused Erica to look around in alarm.

Vicky glanced anxiously over her shoulder toward the organ enclosure. 'Shh…'

They slid silently out through the side door. As soon as they were clear of the grounds, Erica gave an exclamation of relief as she headed up the grassy hill. 'Phew, what a relief. Let's head to the top!'

'Hey, I'm loaded up.' Vicky held up the shopping basket.

Erica reached a flat ledge near the top and turned to wait for her friend to catch up. 'What on earth have you got in there?'

'I took the liberty,' Vicky panted, 'I hope you don't mind. I know we're on a hunt for Jet but…' She pulled out a travel rug and spread it out on the grass.

Erica looked intrigued.

Vicky delved into her bag and brought out cucumber sandwiches. 'And I've been hanging onto this bottle of Chablis.' Vicky filled two plastic cups. They brought them together in a toast, and the two women made a chinking noise. 'It's not every day you're forty.'

Erica laughed, 'I feel more like a kid let out of school.'

They gazed out across the scene. Below the escarpment, the church nestled in the Cauldron Field. Its tower emerged over the tops of the oaks. The steep banks of the ancient hill were swathed with a patchwork quilt of rye grass and clusters of ferns. Here and there White Bryony, Red Campion, and Yellow Flag Iris grew. On the shorter, rabbit-grazed grass of the higher slopes, bees hummed above bunches of buttercups, while over the cow-parsley hover-fly gathered.

'It's good to see you haven't lost your spirit, despite everything,' Vicky said. 'So tell me what happened.'

Erica related how she and Jet had discovered the crystal and then the dog's disappearance. Erica concluded. 'Then I found the bath oil on the doorstep.'

'You must have a secret admirer,' Vicky suggested.

'Hmm… so it wasn't you, then? It was such an unusual fragrance, I didn't mean to, but I poured the whole lot into the bath, it made me feel…' Erica left her sentence hanging, took off her sweater and glanced up at the sun. 'I'm making hay while the sun shines.'

'Not for long though, looks like a storm brewing.' Vicky gestured toward the dark clouds to the west. 'So Erica, what did you make of the service?'

'All this stuff about Adam and Eve, if it wasn't for them we wouldn't be here.'

Vicky nodded.

'If God knew all along we would succumb…' Erica explained, 'why make us susceptible in the first place? Why make the forbidden fruit so gratifying, only to deny anyone the pleasure of it.'

'Perhaps the Bible is saying it's not possible to have freedom without responsibility,' Vicky suggested.

They helped themselves to more wine. Erica lay back and unbuttoned her blouse to expose her midriff to the sun, unaware of the approach from behind of a shadow. She then carried on, in full flow. 'Tell me this. If God invented sex, and made it so much fun to try, why punish Eve when she tried it out…' In slightly slurred tones, Erica continued, 'If it was so damned immoral for them to walk around with no clothes, why did God create us this way in the first place? Such a perverse God doesn't deserve to be trusted an inch.' She undid a final button.

Vicky gave her a subtle nudge and coughed.

Erica continued without taking any notice. 'Why even bother giving Adam the equipment if he wasn't meant to use it…'

'Testosterone can be a bit of an issue at times.' The figure behind took two paces forwards and gave a chuckled grunt. 'Perhaps you might be interpreting the story too literally.'

Vicky laughed nervously and squinted up towards the shape that loomed above, silhouetted against the sun. 'Hello Rodney.' Her tone sounded overly bright. She mopped her brow with a paper napkin. 'Where did you spring from?'

The Reverend beamed. 'I have to apologise for eavesdropping, but your conversation was too intriguing to interrupt.'

Erica wondered how much of the conversation he had overheard and tried to button her blouse. 'The sermon was quite… thought provoking,' she stuttered.

'It's not to be taken literally… it's just a parable. Like most myths, the story says more about the mind of man, than the mind of God. The Bible's like poetry,' Radpole continued, 'it has a universal voice, and speaks to us all on different levels.'

Erica cast a furtive look toward her friend.

Vicky took the hint that she wanted to move the subject on. 'We're celebrating, Rodney.' Vicky offered a cup to the Reverend and shuffled to make space. 'It's Erica's birthday.'

'Ah ha… perhaps just a small one, after all, our Lord must have been partial himself, he did turn the water into wine.' He raised his cup to Erica. 'Or to paraphrase Benjamin Franklin, wine is proof that God wants us to be happy.'

Erica grimaced.

'Your husband had some interesting fundraising ideas,' he continued in buoyant manner. 'I'm also pleased to say he accepted my invitation to have a trial for the village eleven, my dear.'

'He's pretty keen on cricket…' Erica had heard nothing from Simon since the ceremony, and decided to move the topic on. 'Are you on your way to the Maypole, Reverend?'

'Indeed. Unfortunately, I can't stay long with you. Are you joining us?' He beamed.

'We're looking for Erica's dog…' Vicky interjected.

'He's lost?' The Reverend looked concerned.

'Last night, I took him out up on the Hill.' Erica explained.

Radpole frowned. 'I'll pray for his safe return.'

'God knows where he's got to…' Erica had not meant her words to sound quite so literal.

'Things happen up there at night, especially on May Eve.' Rodney swigged the last of his wine. He stood to leave. 'I look forward to continuing our stimulating conversation, soon. You must come to the Ladies' Circle, Mrs Janus, I'm sure the others would enjoy hearing your views.'

Erica started to cough. She had half thought that now the Reverend had heard her doubts, he might no longer have assumed her involvement as a fait accompli.

'Are you all right, my dear?' Radpole rushed to pat her back.

'I'll be fine,' she spluttered.

His hand came to rest on Erica's shoulder and he turned to Vicky. 'The flowers were wonderful today, my dear.'

'My pleasure, Rodney.' Vicky glanced at his arm around Erica. 'We'll have to hurry, Erica, there's rain on the way.'

'Take care you two.' He gave a wave. 'I'd better hurry too, or it'll be all over.' He sprang off, up toward the summit.

Erica began to hiccup and held her breath until the Reverend was out of sight, whereupon the two women fell into a fit of giggles.

Spots of rain began to land. Erica became anxious. 'Come on, Vicky let's look for Jet, before it gets too heavy.'

They hurriedly packed away the picnic things.

'We'll head for the Ladypool.'

The path to the pool encircled the north side of the Hill. Every few yards they shouted the dog's name. They gathered speed as the shower grew in intensity.

'We're not dressed for rain.' Vicky became uneasy. 'We'll need to take shelter.'

St Catherine's Chapel was part of an old friary and nestled next to the Ladypool in a hidden fold of the wooded landscape. When they reached its walls, it was raining hard. For a few minutes, they took refuge under the broad eaves of a large oak.

'Sam told me scholars believe the Romans thought the ancients worshipped Catherine, that's why this chapel is named after her. But he says what the ancients were saying were the words Cader rhyn, and that's hill throne in the old Celtic language.'

'Ahh, of course, it must be like Cader Idris, that means Arthur's Seat,' Erica agreed. 'Whatever the derivation it's certainly an ancient place.'

'On the first day of Spring in the old days,' Vicky continued, 'the young men paraded from the top, while the women started at the chapel, to spiral up the path.' She paused.

Erica listened, entranced.

'I needn't say what happened when they met,' Vicky said.

'Then, it's a good job we only met Rodney en route,' Erica joked. The symbolism began to excite her. She made a spiral shape in the air with her finger and grinned. 'One could almost believe it goes to heaven.'

'Except that it leads to the Hell,' Vicky looked sad and her gaze fell down to the earth.

Erica guessed Vicky was thinking of Rowan and she waited a few seconds before continuing in a different vein. 'I was inspired in the service this morning.' Erica said. 'I realised something - the words; spring, spiral, spire, and spirit - they're all linked.'

'You should be helping Rodney write his sermons.' Vicky said and mustered a chuckle.

Erica nodded toward the high rocks behind the Ladypool. 'That's where Jet disappeared, up there. Come on; the rain's gone off.' Erica scrambled on ahead.

They struggled up the steep face. After several scrapes, Erica helped Vicky haul herself up onto the topmost ledge. Out of breath, they fought through the undergrowth of ferns and stooped into the shelter of the cleft. Vicky crouched next to Erica and began to protest at the state of her mud-spattered clothes.

'Shh…' Erica interrupted her, 'listen.' They squatted in silence. They could hear a faint, distant bubbling.

'The source of the Awen is meant to be here somewhere. Is this where you found the crystal?' Vicky quizzed.

Erica nodded and looked up at Vicky, uneasily. 'Promise not to say a word, or there'll be all sorts poking around up here.'

'I'll not mention it.' Vicky pointed into the cave. 'These are workings from the days when they mined for silver.'

Erica knelt down to look at something on the rock-face. 'Amazing...' she exclaimed. In the shadows, the carved outline of a shape no bigger than a handprint was just discernable. 'The same sign was in the church window and on the bath oil,' Erica declared. 'It must be quite old.'

Vicky leant over to study it. 'A diamond around a cross - it must mean something, pilgrims sometimes used symbols to mark special places.'

'Come on, the rain's gone off.' Erica reached out to help Vicky clamber down and they slithered back to the edge of the pool, where for a minute, they stopped and gazed.

'Over the years,' Vicky said, 'people have claimed to have seen a beautiful young woman with flowers in her hair. Rodney's even written about the myth.'

'Perhaps she used to tease the friars at St Catherine's and give them lustful thoughts,' suggested Erica. She stared into the circle of darkness. 'Have you ever seen her?'

'No, but Will declares he has... a lady in white, a priestess.'

'A priestess...' Erica whispered. She stood motionless and stared across the shimmering surface. Drops of rain created a lattice, like woven lace. The echo of a faint murmur mingled with the pitter-patter of raindrops landing upon the water...

Icera... Icera... Icera...

****

Sam let his eyes scan the beauty of the figure in white. *Primavera* was his favourite Botticelli. The reproduction hung on the wall of his Emporium. He held the receiver and smiled. 'So Chris, you're coming to England tomorrow? One of these days we'll have to meet up and you can bring me up to date with quantum physics. It'll be just like the old days, but don't try to tie me up in knots with your string theory.'

On the other end of the phone, Chris chuckled. 'All we seek is to reach the next rung on the ladder.'

'My friend,' Sam said, 'it is indeed the staircase to the stars...'

Chapter 13

The Invitation

ERICA LED VICKY THROUGH the gateway of Corner Cottage. Simon's silver BMW sat in the drive.

'Perhaps he's found a lady-friend.'

Vicky's comment caused Erica to stop dead.

Vicky looked uncomfortable. 'Jet, I meant.'

Erica sighed and closed the front door behind them. 'Let's call it a day. I feel a bit woozy. Come upstairs and we'll change.'

They entered the bedroom and Erica nodded toward the crystal.

Vicky looked in silent amazement and she held it up to the window. Her eyes closed and she disappeared into her own thoughts. After a minute, Erica watched Vicky's dreamy expression suddenly change and Vicky surfaced from her trance-like state. She glanced across to Erica. 'I saw Rowan. He used to talk about a stone.' Vicky continued in a matter-of-fact tone. 'It looks like quartz. Sam might know what it is,' she suggested. 'I'll phone him, if you like?'

'We better get out of these wet things, first. Do you want a shower?' Erica asked.

'I just need to dry off.'

'Use this...' Erica tossed Vicky a dressing gown and a towel and Erica headed for the bathroom.

The noise of the shower masked the sound of footsteps on the stairs. The bedroom door opened. 'Did you find your...' The sight of a semi-clad woman halted Simon in his tracks. 'Sorry, I didn't realise...' he spluttered.

Vicky threw the robe around her. 'Erica's in the shower, we got drenched, looking for Jet,' she blurted in a burst.

Simon glanced at the pile of wet clothes lying on the bed and regained his composure. 'Looks like you could do with warming up, I'll make some coffee.'

The bathroom door opened and Erica frowned at her husband. 'Simon, this is Vicky, and we're changing.'

'I see you've been celebrating.' He glanced at the empty bottle of Chablis. Then, he strode over to the crystal on the windowsill. 'A birthday present?'

Erica was annoyed. She wondered if she was going to receive a gift from Simon this year. 'Coffee, Simon...'

'Pleased to meet you, Vicky.' He held out the crystal toward her and eyed it at arm's length. 'Fine body,' he grinned, 'and nice... what is it they call the fault lines... cleavage?'

'Simon... coffee.' Erica became more irritated.

'Your present.' Simon nodded toward the wardrobe. 'It's in there, you can share it with Sarah, then you won't be fighting over mine.'

Erica poked her head into the closet and saw the computer. 'Thanks, how practical...' She managed a half-hearted smile. 'Better leave it till Sarah's here.' Erica knew her daughter would not want to share. 'Simon, coffee.'

Simon looked slightly puzzled at her lack of enthusiasm and turned to Vicky. 'Brazilian?'

'Um,' Vicky said, uncertainly. 'Ahh coffee, yes, of course, thank you.'

A few minutes later, the two women entered the kitchen. Simon sauntered over to Vicky with a cup. 'This should warm you up...' He turned to Erica. 'The pot's on the stove.'

Vicky nodded her thanks to Simon. 'I'll give my uncle a ring, if I may? He's going to have a look at the crystal for Erica,' she explained.

'Is he in the trade, then?' Simon asked.

'He owns the Emporium.'

'Ah, the Old Prof, that's what everyone calls him down the Green Man.'

'That's him, Sam's always been interested in crystals.' Vicky dialled. She explained the situation to her uncle and then announced to Erica, 'One o'clock tomorrow ok...'

The letterbox rattled. Through the kitchen window, Erica noticed the figure of Kneebone disappearing down the path.

Simon returned from the hall holding a postcard of St Michael's. 'It's an invitation to tea at the Manse, next Sunday.'

Vicky nodded, 'I've had one too.'

Simon turned to Vicky with a smile. 'Not to be missed, then.'

Vicky finished her cup, and proposed to head back. 'My Morris is at the church.'

'I'll give you a lift.' Simon jangled his keys at Vicky. 'I want to nip in to see Rodney.' He glanced, archly, at his wife. 'I'll come back for you, that'll give you time to recover from the Chablis, before you drop me off at the station. See you soon, my dear.'

Erica eyed him. 'That's very kind, Simon.' Why had he suddenly discovered a newfound enthusiasm for Vicar's tea parties? 'I've arranged to pick up Sarah from Dorchester.'

One hour later, Erica was reversing Simon out of the drive. The BMW scraped the gatepost.

'For God's sake!' Simon threw down the Sunday paper, 'I'll drive,' he demanded.

Erica mopped her brow. 'I'll be fine.' Gingerly, she continued down the lane.

Simon huffed and buried his head in the paper.

After a few minutes, Erica asked, 'Simon, do you know anything about a bottle of bath essence I discovered on the doorstep?'

'A present eh? Probably Rodney.'

'Nonsense.' She knew Simon was winding her up.

'He mentioned he'd met you two on the Hill.' Simon chuckled. 'Rumour has it he's got a bit of a soft spot for the ladies… Still, better that, than a penchant for choirboys.'

The freckled lad from the church service came into Erica's mind.

A tractor suddenly emerged from a field. 'Watch out!' Simon exclaimed.

They veered over onto the verge.

'What's up with you today…' Simon snorted. After a few moments, he returned to the paper. 'That Chablis must have gone to your head.'

They fell into an uneasy silence. As she did every Sunday afternoon, Erica went into automatic mode and passed the time by rewinding the previous twenty-four hours - the Horned monster, finding the crystal, losing Jet. Then, images from the night began to invade - Wyllow… the flames of the fires reflected in his eyes. The car turned into the station forecourt. Before she knew it, a shock of tousled blond hair bobbed out in front. It was him … it was Wyllow!

'Look out!' Simon grabbed the steering wheel and they swerved. Erica forced her foot onto the floor. There was a screech of brakes.

CHAPTER 14

The Bright Fire

SARAH RAN UP AND stood at the open car window. '…Are you OK mum?'

'We're all right.' Simon barked. 'God knows what's wrong with your mum. Thank god no-one's hurt. That's the third near miss today and I'm late.' He grabbed his briefcase from the back seat and strode off for the London train.

Erica emerged from the car looking dazed and stared blankly, in front of her. Where had the blond lad gone?

'Come on mum, you need a break, let's go for a coffee.' Sarah linked arms with her mother and they headed towards the buffet. 'I've fallen in love.'

Erica peered in the direction the lad had been walking.

'I'm in love,' Sarah repeated, dreamily.

She turned to her daughter and brought her to a stop. 'What are you saying… who with?' Erica pictured the long tousled blond locks, bobbing in front of her.

Sarah giggled. 'He's so hunky.'

'Who?' she asked in exasperation.

'…Johnny Depp, of course.'

Her mother breathed out a sigh. She stared at Sarah's jeans. 'Don't tell me you got that from going to the cinema?'

'Don't panic mum, it's just a bit of mud, that's all.'

When they arrived home, there was still no sign of Jet.

Sarah tried to reassure her. 'He'll find his own way back sooner or later, stop worrying, mum.'

Sarah's tone took Erica slightly aback. Why did her daughter seem so unperturbed, by the loss of the dog? She handed Sarah her birthday present. 'Happy birthday, dear.'

Sarah unwrapped it. 'Thanks mum, it's great…' She slipped the bracelet onto her wrist.

Erica detected a hint of disappointment in her daughter's voice. In the end, it had been a last minute choice, and she wished now she had chosen something different.

'Happy birthday, Mum.' Sarah gave her mother a package wrapped in gold.

Erica was taken aback. It was the same wrapping paper as the bath essence. 'Thank you, darling.' She took out a small octagonal bottle. 'What a strange shape!'

'It's a special aromatic oil,' Sarah said.

Erica unscrewed the cap and lifted the bottle to her nose. 'It smells just like my bath oil.' Then, she noticed the logo on the label. 'Where did you get this?'

'Just someone in the village.' Sarah said.

'Do they make these fragrances here? A package like this was left on the doorstep last night.'

Sarah changed the subject. 'Where's dad's pressie?'

Her mother led her daughter upstairs to the computer.

Sarah sat down in the dressing room and tapped some keys. 'Cool, it's hooked up. We could always have it alternate evenings...' Sarah suggested and stifled a yawn.

Her mother was surprised and gratified that it seemed to find favour with Sarah. 'You look tired, darling. These sleepovers seem to become hangovers.'

'I don't do sleepovers, they're for kids.' Sarah rose indignantly from the stool. She was heading for the door when her expression changed. She raced over to the crystal and held the crystal aloft. 'I love it.' Light from the window refracted onto her face into a patchwork of blue and indigo. The colours glinted in her eyes. 'Where did you find it? It's from another world.'

Erica shared her excitement. 'It's not precious like a diamond, but I've the feeling it's quite special.'

'It's beautiful... mysterious. It feels powerful. Can you feel it mum, when you hold it?' Sarah caressed it in both hands. 'Did someone give it to you?' she asked.

'Jet and I found it,' Erica hesitated, 'near the Ladypool.'

'That place is magic,' Sarah whispered and a look of serenity fell over her face.

They both fell silent. After a few moments, Erica announced, 'Listen, I've been thinking, I'd like to give you the crystal for your birthday.'

'Mum, brilliant! We've shared one present, so we'll share this one too.'

As Sarah took the crystal up to her room, her mother smiled and called after her, 'Don't forget you have to be up early for college tomorrow.'

An hour later, Sarah's homework lay half-finished on the desk. She had fallen asleep on the bed. Erica retrieved the crystal from her daughter's hands, covered her with the duvet, and turned off the light.

In her own room, Erica changed into her nightclothes. She lit the burner and poured some liquid out from the bottle. The room filled with the heady mixture of strange woodland aromas. The potent potpourri permeated her senses.

The new computer seemed to log in, automatically. A combination appeared on the screen – 34125 and a female voice announced, 'You have mail.'

'Strange, I didn't even set a password…' she saw the name on the screen and her heart raced. Perplexed, she read aloud the waiting mail message. 'We hoped you enjoyed your bath, Wyllow.'

She typed a reply to the address - 'You sent the bath essence?'

Immediately, a chime announced a reply. 'Come to the Cernstone, bring the crystal.'

She typed, 'Do you mean the Hell Stone?' She was bewildered and amazed - the crystal… how did he know about that?

'Yes,' came the reply, 'at midnight.'

Her sense told her not to follow, but her instinct told her otherwise. She threw on her robe and placed the crystal in her pocket.

It should have taken a full half hour to reach the open heath, yet, propelled by anticipation, only minutes seemed to have passed before Erica felt the soft, springy turf under her feet.

The scene ahead mirrored images from the visions of the previous night, but tonight, all her senses were alive. She could feel the heat, smell the wood smoke, and hear the crackle of the fires. This was no fantasy, this was happening in front of her eyes.

She approached the summit, and the glow from two fires became visible through the trees. Flames lit up the smoke as fierce spits sparked out from the embers. Between the flames, stood the Altar, the round flat rock, two paces across. Six figures huddled around it, illuminated in a circle. A seventh figure a tall and slender came toward her. The frame - the tousled blond hair, the glint in his eyes - she recognised its familiar masculine form.

'Wyllow.' He offered her a sheepskin.

'Welcome…' the rest of the group echoed.

From their manner, she guessed the others were girls in their late teens. They wore rough woven cloaks over red silk gowns. She tried to catch sight of their faces under their hoods. Some seemed curiously familiar. Perhaps she had seen them around the village.

A black shadow bounded over. 'Jet!' She threw her arms around him. He pawed and licked her. 'Where have you been?' At last, her dog was next to her again, now she would not leave his side. She wrapped the rug around her, and joined the group sitting on their animal skins.

'This is so strange, last night, I was here…' She was about to enter into an explanation of what she had witnessed in her dream but she stopped herself. Why was Jet here? Just who was Wyllow? How could this be happening?

A girl with a streak of red in her hair held out a bowl. 'Homemade shroom soup? Fruits of the forest…'

An aroma of herbs and dank earth met Erica's nostrils. Despite the smeared ochre on the girls face Erica felt she knew her. 'Aren't you Dee, Beebee's girl?'

The girl looked uneasy. 'My name's Eed.'

Erica supped the comforting brew. The firelight illuminated their faces. It was not long before the group were stretched out in front of the fires. Erica finished the broth and she too began to feel mellow. It all seemed so natural - to be there, out on the Hill, in the small hours of the night.

Wyllow began to relate a story. 'Ten winters ago, before my father entered the Otherworld, through the doorway of dreams, he talked of a stone.' Wyllow paused, and looked to Erica. 'He named it after an ancient priestess. He called it the Icera Stone.'

At the centre of the Altar, Erica noticed a cup-shaped indentation. She realised what had to be done. She took the crystal from her pocket, held the stone by the tips of her fingers, and placed the crystal in the hollow. It fitted exactly, as though it were a mount for a jewel.

'Hendasfolk,' Wyllow proclaimed, 'behold…'

The fires cast shadows and reflections upon their faces. Cradled in the hollow at the centre, in the light from the two fires, the crystal glowed. An interplay of blue and yellow anointed the Altar, and danced across its flat surface like a fountain in a pool. The group stared, spellbound. The apex of the crystal aligned along the direction of the Cursus.

Wyllow held up a burning torch and made the sign of a diamond in which he formed a cross. 'Four within one; air, fire, earth, and water,' he proclaimed. 'From air born of fire in a womb of stone, water is your blood.' Then, he spoke softly. '**Star goddess, Icera,** we open our minds to love.'

The group began to intone a word. As sharp as frost, yet soft as summer's day their voices united. 'Ice-era... I-cera... Icera...' The mantra gained pace until it reached a crescendo.

Erica became lost in the sound, her eyelids drooped... and she fell into a deep sleep.

****

At three thousand feet, above the South Coast of England, the transatlantic Boeing was nearing the end of the flight. Dr Christopher Credus had a far-away look in his eyes. In the subdued light, the screen saver kicked in and a blue translucent pyramid slowly rotated on his laptop computer. He stared out of the porthole into the night sky; there shone the distant star, surrounded by her six sisters... beckoning.

Chris strained to see if he could recognise anything in the landscape - he knew he was somewhere near the place of his birth. Far below, two lonely isolated specks of light, surrounded by a sea of darkness, flickered.

He returned his gaze to the image on the screen. A sense of wonder came over him - the same feeling he had first experienced as a twenty-two year old post-graduate student - the room at Cambridge framed by the ivy-covered stone of a gothic arched window. His tutor, Sam Haines, sketched on the board a tetrahedron, the molecular structure of a crystal of silicone. He remembered how he had felt - how he had been overcome by a sense of intense anticipation, as though, for the first time, a secret door had opened and another world revealed. He had taken a step over the threshold to begin a journey of discovery and, from then, not looked back. That day, twenty years ago, for the first time, he had fully comprehended the true nature of mathematics... and it had been beautiful.

He recalled his professor's words. 'If you want to learn about nature, you must understand the language she speaks.'

'The language she speaks...' he repeated the words in a whisper. He looked out into the darkness once more, through the window to the stars... something was about to be revealed - something no less than the mind of god.

CHAPTER 15

The Emporium

SOMETHING HOT AND WET pushed against Erica's neck causing her heart to rush. Her eyes squinted into the sunlight. A sense of relief flooded over her. Jet lay beside her on top of her duvet. She petted and stroked her dog and, for a moment, she felt everything was back to normal, but then, an un-nerving realisation took hold. It felt like ants were crawling over her legs. She looked down. Encrusted mud spattered her limbs.

For a few minutes, she tried to piece together the fragments of the night. She stared at her muddy mules by her side. Try as she might, she could not recall returning to her bed.

She stood up and steadied herself against the wall. The room turned like a carousel. How could she have a hangover? She had no recollection of taking anything stronger than soup. 'Shroom soup… shroom soup… shroom soup…' her last memory of the night echoed around her head.

She staggered towards her daughter's room and shouted from the landing. 'Sarah, wake up, he's come back. Isn't it fantastic? Goodness knows what he's been up to since Saturday night. It's time you got up, we've overslept, it's eight o'clock already, I feel like I've got a hangover.'

A groan came from under the bedclothes. 'Monday eughh…'

Before her daughter could surface, Erica rushed through to the bathroom. She stared across at the mirror. The face that gazed back had charcoaled cheeks covered in ochre, and tousled locks. She turned the shower up high to wash away the evidence of the night, when she realised... her ammonite - it was no longer around her neck.

'Sorry mum, I've missed the bus, can you drive me?'

Erica hesitated before she took the car keys off the hook - she was still feeling woozy and had a drink of water. She made sure Jet came with them. 'I wonder where he got to...'

Sarah was philosophical. 'I said he'd turn up.'

'Have you seen my ammonite?'

'No mum, but I have this.' Her daughter said, earnestly. 'Look after it, won't you.' She handed her mother the crystal.

****

Monday morning for Simon came with an early wake up call from the party's press secretary. 'What... where?' Simon asked, bleary eyed. 'I haven't approved of any photo of me!' he fumed.

Simon rushed to the newsagent in Streatham High Road. There for all to see, sprawled out on his backside in the cowpat was Simon. The picture was on the front page of every tabloid. He scowled at the headlines - Janus Kicks Up a Stink... Janus on his Anus... It gets Hot and Sticky for Janus. He scooped up an armful of newspapers.

The Indian proprietor grinned at him from behind the counter. 'For you, Mr Janus, they're free, now you're so famous!'

****

In the distance, St Michael's clock struck one. The jangle of the shop doorbell echoed a reply and continued to repeat inside Erica's head. That morning, she had been the butt of a heated phone call from her husband over coverage in the press and she was not feeling together. She peered into the gloom of the dusty interior. A scene bathed in muted shadows of browns and greys lay before her.

A cultured, masculine voice addressed her from the darkness somewhere within. 'Would you be kind enough to turn the sign on the door?'

Erica switched the open sign to closed and made her way hesitantly towards the rear of the Emporium. She negotiated her way around several large Chinese vases, collided into an art nouveau hat stand, and fell into the outstretched arms of a stuffed bear.

'Are you all right?' came the voice. 'You seem a little unsteady.'

She tried to make light of her wooziness. 'It was so bright outside,' she explained.

A silhouette sat hunched behind a desk. The figure stood up and turned toward her. 'I'm used to it in here.' He switched on the desk lamp.

Now, she could see him clearly, a short stocky man with white hair and a bushy moustache. He wore a bright red waistcoat, tartan check shirt with a bow tie. He gestured across the walnut desk to a vacant chair. 'Please take a seat, Mrs Janus, I'm Sam Haines.'

'Erica…' she said. They shook hands and she flopped into the seat.

He eased back and peered over his half-moon glasses. 'Congratulations.'

'You mean today's paper.' She attempted to put in check her feeling of annoyance at her husband's antics.

'It's the first time Witchbury has ever made the front-page, but no,' he smiled, 'I was referring to your birthday.'

'I'm not feeling quite with-it today.' Erica shook her head in response. 'Simon was absolutely livid this morning.'

'He'll certainly be the talk of the village,' Sam agreed. 'He made quite a splash, if a muddy one.'

Erica felt more at ease and chuckled at Sam making light of the matter. She decided it best to change tack. She looked around and noticed a familiar image on the wall. 'I see you like Botticelli.'

'The Primavera.' Sam turned to look at the reproduction. 'I sometimes wish I had been an artist rather than a scientist.'

Erica sensed she could be open with Sam. 'Both art and science are about being in harmony with nature.'

'So true.' Sam studied her. 'I understand, from my niece, you've got something interesting to show me.'

From her shopping bag, Erica unwrapped the find. She looked at him, hopefully. 'Vicky suggested you might be able to help identify it.'

His bushy eyebrows shot up. He took out a magnifying glass from the drawer, and adjusted the lamp.

She watched his expression. 'Is it valuable?'

He pushed his spectacles to the end of his round nose and for a few moments did not speak. 'Where did you get it?' he asked.

'I was out with my dog on Saturday night, on the Oakenland... what do you think it is?'

'It's certainly most unusual,' he replied in a measured tone. 'It's a little like Tetrahedrite, but this crystal is far too large for it to be that. I've never seen one exactly like this before.' He paused again and took out a pencil from his drawer. 'This form suggests a type of quartz. The basic molecular structure consists of one central atom of silicon, surrounded by four oxygen atoms.' Sam began to draw a pyramid.

'Can you see how closely the stone reflects the fundamental molecular structure - the four-faced pyramid with a triangular base?'

'Amazing,' Erica said. She looked a little bewildered. 'I'm sorry, tetrawhat...?'

Sam glanced at Erica's glazed expression. 'Perhaps a coffee?' He reached round to the shelf behind him and poured the liquid, as black as liquorice, into two cups. 'There's always some on the go.'

She took a sip. It acted as an instant antidote. Erica studied the drawing. 'So does that make it rare?'

'An exciting find, indeed... Certain geometrical formations can be highly valued by collectors and this one's exceptional. The foiled inclusion divides the stone into two equal pieces... most compelling.' Sam studied it with a magnifying glass.

Erica nodded. 'So it is natural?'

'During formation air pockets in a rock can protect a crystal's growth from impurities. Just like a pearl within a shell, but how this could form so perfectly is beyond me.' Sam paused then he looked over to Erica. 'I do know someone however who has a great deal more knowledge about crystals than I do. He was my postgraduate student at Cambridge. He's based in North Carolina nowadays, but he happens to be over in this country at the moment to give a lecture at Cambridge on Friday.'

Erica was doubtful. 'I don't know... it's my daughter, she's rather attached to it... I'd prefer not to send it away.'

Sam considered the matter for a few seconds. 'I'll email photographs.' He peered at her over his glasses. 'Leave it with me, I'll let you know what he says.' The professor held up the crystal to the light and began to reminisce. 'Chris Credus and I used to have many late night discussions about all the things still left to discover. We used to speculate about many things - evolution, intelligent design, fossils...' Sam noticed Erica clutching at her neck. 'Are you all right?'

Erica faltered. 'I've lost a necklace that was rather important to me.' Her eyes glazed over.

'Oh dear... sentimental value?' Sam asked.

'It was just something someone gave me once.' Erica became pensive.

'Hold on, I have a recent issue of the New Scientist.' Sam rifled through his desk drawer, took out the magazine, and pointed to an article entitled the Quantum Computer. 'That's Dr Credus. He's quite charismatic isn't he?'

Erica gazed at the small photo of a clean-shaven man wearing a blue check, country-style shirt. How intense and bright were his eyes. 'I don't know why, professor, but Dr Credus looks somehow familiar. May I borrow this?'

CHAPTER 16
The Photograph

'Where's the crystal, Mum?'

It had been the first question Sarah asked that afternoon when she arrived home from Sixth Form College.

'With Vicky's uncle; I left it with him this morning.'

'You said you wouldn't.'

'I'm picking it up tomorrow. He's only photographing it.'

Sarah glared at her mother, grabbed her school bag and stormed off in frustration.

The next morning when Erica awoke, her eyes opened to an insistent ringing. Images from a dream briefly lingered - a meteor falling to earth and woman in white. She rushed downstairs to answer the phone. It was Sam.

'He wants to see it? That sounds brilliant... but...' Erica felt anxious. 'The thing is, it's my daughter... she's become so attached to it. I don't really want to let it out of my sight.'

'No problem,' Sam insisted. 'He's invited us both to his lecture, we can take it to him in person.'

'That would be wonderful... but...'

Sam jumped in. 'It'll give me the chance to meet some of my old Cambridge colleagues, and we don't have that much time, he's going back to the States on Monday.'

The New Scientist article lay open on the desk. She looked again at his photo. Something in the Chris Credus's eyes spoke to her. 'Ok Sam, that would be great.'

Sam held up the crystal to the lamp and gazed into the inner reflections. 'Excellent, we'll leave for Cambridge on Thursday.'

Erica put the receiver slowly down. She would have to find a way to placate Sarah, somehow.

****

The librarian looked up from the desk in surprise. 'You're an early bird Mrs Janus.'

Erica girded herself. She was expecting Beebee to be wound up over the publicity given to Simon at the Beltane ceremony. 'Good morning,' Erica said, brightly. 'It's a lovely Spring day. I did try to warn him, but you know how men are.'

'Obdurate, most of them, Mrs Janus,' she whispered.

Beebee did not seem her usual self. Other matters seemed to be pressing on the librarian's mind and Erica tried to be conciliatory. 'I understand more about the tradition now. Pardon my questions the other day.'

It was a few moments before Beebee responded. 'You're lucky I'm here today. It's my girl Dee,' she faltered. 'Took bad, yesterday, she was - something she ate. I been at the hospital most of the night.' Beebee gestured a thrusting action with her arm. 'They had to pump her out.'

'How awful.' A fleeting notion of Shroom soup came into Erica's mind and a sense of disquiet overtook her. 'How is she now?'

'Back home in bed.' Beebee composed herself and adopted a more formal tone. 'Now, what can we help you with today, Mrs Janus?'

'I do hope she'll be back at college tomorrow.' Erica sympathised and had to think why she had come before responding. 'I'm looking for information, about - the Lady in White.'

Beebee gave a smile of recognition. 'I think Rodney's written something about her. There's a box out the back for local folklore... I won't be a sec...'

Erica watched through the stock room door as Beebee wobbled precariously on top of a pair of library steps.

A few minutes later, with much huffing and puffing, she returned to the counter clutching a shoebox from which she extracted a small pamphlet. 'He wrote it shortly after he came to the parish.'

Erica felt thankful that the librarian seemed more approachable than on previous occasions. 'What a treasure you are, Beebee, would you mind if I borrowed it?'

'It's the copyright of the Reverend.'

Erica persisted, 'I'll mention how helpful you've been when I see him.'

Beebee hesitated. 'As it's you, Mrs Janus.' She copied the pamphlet and handed over the pages.

'Please do call me Erica, and thank you so much for all your help, you're an absolute mine of information.'

Beebee looked pleased.

When she reached her car, Erica studied the pamphlet with as much concentration as she could muster. The identity of the Lady in White ranged from the Virgin Mary to a Roman Goddess. She was not surprised to find that the Reverend seemed to have given most credence to the story of St Catherine, but in small print at the end, in an added footnote, she read aloud, 'There is also the vestige of a story that links a Bronze Age priestess with the protection of the purity of the water.'

****

Thursday morning, Sam drove Erica to Dorchester. The ten o'clock London train was half empty and they sat at facing window seats. They had booked rooms for the night in a hotel in Cambridge. They were to meet Chris Credus the following day, after his lecture. She was pleased to be able to spend time away from home and allow some thinking space to get a perspective on her life. It would also provide the opportunity to quiz Vicky's uncle. When the train was underway, she turned to him. 'Sam, I meant to show you this before.' She took out the brooch from her bag.

Instantly, a look of recognition flashed across Sam's face. 'Where did you get this?'

'My daughter was given it as a present,' Erica said. 'The clip's broken. Vicky wondered if you could mend it.'

Sam was bowled over. 'By rights this should be in the British Museum.' He paused. 'I have to confess I've seen it once before.'

'You have?' Erica was amazed.

'It belonged to Will's father, he showed it to me once,' Sam explained. 'He called it the Beltane Brooch.'

'The Beltane Brooch…' Erica repeated. 'Strange…' She looked puzzled. 'Vicky didn't mention it.'

'He was rather secretive over some things. Toward the end, Rowan used to relate more to their son, Will.' Sam's expression became briefly regretful, before he continued. 'If I'm right, it's probably over three thousand years old. I suggest we get it checked out by the museum in Dorchester when we get back from Cambridge.'

'Sam,' Erica put the brooch back in her bag, 'I need to know something…'

He looked at her enquiringly.

'Will's father, how did he die?'

Sam hesitated and shook his head. 'Tragic… he fell from Devil's Drop.'

Erica turned ashen.

Sam nodded. 'Onto the Portal Stone.'

'How awful, it must have affected Vicky, terribly.'

Sam looked sombre. 'I feel she's never really recovered.'

'What about Will?' she asked.

'He's caught up in the whole Celtic thing - gone off the rails, recently. To tell you the truth, he's disappointed me. I tried to be a father to him, not that I could replace Rowan. I had great hopes that Will might make a brilliant scientist one day.'

'Perhaps it's just temporary, you know what they're like at that age.'

Sam shook his head. 'He's become more wrapped up in magic than science.'

Erica reflected, 'Who was it who said any sufficiently advanced technology is indistinguishable from magic?'

Sam looked impressed. 'Arthur C. Clarke,' he answered. 'I like to think, perhaps one day, science and magic will meet.'

In London, they transferred via the tube to Kings Cross. They bought packed lunches from the buffet and settled down at an empty table on the Cambridge train. 'Do excuse me,' Sam said, 'it's a habit of mine.' He took out the Times and a pen and began the crossword.

After a few minutes, Erica spread out a napkin on the table. 'Sam,' she asked, 'may I borrow your pen? It's my turn to draw.'

He handed her the pen and she began to sketch. 'Do you recognise this? It was in the stained glass in the church.'

Sam studied her diagram. 'Hmm… a cross within a diamond - there are similarities to symbols in early alchemy.' He thought for a while. 'It's pure speculation but it might stand for the four ancient elements.'

Erica was intrigued.

Sam pointed to the base. 'These could be Earth and water,' he suggested, 'And air and fire could be the upper triangles.

'Fascinating, and the diamond?' asked Erica.

'The sum of its parts, the unity - the force that binds all others, the fifth element.'

'The Quintessence…' Erica stated.

'Quite so.' Sam smiled. Soon, his eyes closed.

Erica studied the drawing. Something made her take the crystal from the wooden box in her bag. She placed it on the napkin. For a while, she lost herself in a daydream inside its geometry. Suddenly, a ray of sunlight shone through a gap in the cloud and projected a silhouette onto the drawing. The pattern of the translucent blue shadow from the crystal fell over the sketch - it matched exactly. Erica shouted in astonishment. 'Sam, wake up! Quick, before it goes...'

For a second, Sam rubbed his eyes in amazement. Then, the train entered a tunnel and the image was lost.

****

Not until she was ready for bed, in the Cambridge hotel, did Erica finally find time to study the article in the New Scientist. The technicalities mostly went over her head but, when she switched off the light and closed her eyes to let her dreams take flight, all she could see she was the man with the sparkling eyes. 'What has drawn me here, Dr Credus? What was it Sam said - perhaps one day science and magic will meet?'

CHAPTER 17

The Lecture

THE LECTURE THEATRE BUZZED with anticipation. Erica carried the canvas holdall above the heads of the people on the back row. She and Sam squeezed along to sit in the last two remaining seats.

Dr Credus wore a white cotton shirt open at the collar, the sleeves were partly rolled-up over his sun-tanned arms, and his faded blue Levis revealed a slim, athletic frame. Energized but calm, he walked up to the lectern and brushed back his long dark hair. From a soft leather travel bag, he removed his laptop computer and plugged it into a slot on the podium. With a hint of humour, his eyes scanned the audience. He was a star-turn in Cambridge and, returning to his academic roots, he always felt inspired. For a few seconds, he stood with his head bowed until the audience settled.

The lights dimmed; the opening notes of the theme from 2001 played at full volume, and the audience fell silent. Dr Credus raised his head. 'Two icons - they have something in common...' The audience gazed at the image on the screen, the sun rose from behind the Heelstone at Stonehenge. Superimposed over this an equation gradually came into view... $E=mc^2$. The only noise in the lecture theatre was the hiss of air through the ventilation grills. 'If there are any of you left at the end of my talk, I'll let you know what secret the two symbols share.'

He smiled at the muffled groans, and continued. 'One hundred years ago, Max Planck conceived of the quantum. He could not have predicted his theories would lead, a generation later, to atom bombs over Japan and change our world forever. When scientists gathered at Los Alamos for the Manhattan Project, they were working towards a common goal. Two generations on, we also have an agreed objective… Soon, silicon will be dead meat. Moore, will be no more.'

He scanned his audience for a reaction. A mixture of undergraduates, research scientists and professors faced him. Those who had recognised the allusion to the well-known computer law chuckled at his play on words.

'What is the potential prize… to find a successor to silicon, a computer architecture capable of factorising encryption codes, which today's computers would take years to decode. Such a computer would have the power to access your credit card, or crack the aiming code for any nuclear device. This is the subject of my talk today - the Quantum Computer.'

The audience sat in rapt silence.

'So, how might such a computer work?' The screen changed to a laser beam, hitting a crystal.

'Just as different parts of a human brain can be stimulated by electricity, different frequencies of light can be used to excite a molecular array.'

Projected on the screen, a drawing of a flat earth appeared. 'Today's chip is two-dimensional. If brains were flat, each would need to occupy an area about this big.' The image zoomed into a map of the UK. 'That wouldn't leave us much room to have fun. So, what about a three-dimensional computer brain with something other than pulses of electrons travelling along bits of copper?'

He looked around. 'What's the fastest thing we know?'

Like a schoolboy in a classroom Sam threw up his hand. 'Light,' he shouted.

Chris immediately recognised his old friend. 'Correct professor.' He noticed the woman next to Sam and his heart missed a beat. Her face seemed to stir some distant memory. He was forced to pause to regain his composure. After a few seconds, he continued. 'And the smallest quantity of light is?'

A hand at the front shot up.

Chris spotted him. 'Yes, the young man with the scarf?'

'A photon...' He replied, tentatively.

'Quite correct, and has anyone ever thought how strange it is that something so small, has no problem with the journey from the other side the universe without even a medium to travel in?' Chris left the question hanging.

'Newton demonstrated, how that same photon, can be slowed down by a substance as simple as water.' The slide changed to a rainbow.

'Light travels in a line, about as straight as a Physics Fresher heading for the bar after one of my lectures... to divert his path would require a huge pull of gravity... something like this.' A projection of a Black Hole came up before them.

He paused for a ripple of laughter to die down. 'Black hole generators are rare, so what substance would enable us to control photons?'

The theme from James Bond, Diamonds are Forever, struck up. 'You got it.' An image of a blue gemstone appeared. 'The imprint of the pattern of photons remains stored, captured in the spin states of the axes of rotation of the atoms in crystals.'

A black and white photo of a young boy with antique headset appeared on the screen. 'Some of you may have heard of a crystal set. When I was a kid of ten, I had my first germanium crystal wireless set.'

The screen changed to show a molecule, illustrated by a three-dimensional array of tiny spheres. 'This is germanium quartz. NASA manufactured this one in zero gravity space, last year. The molecules are far apart. The photons can reach their destinations along parallel tramlines. It's possible to alter the spin of molecules to form patterns.' Chris peered at the young man on the front row who was fidgeting with his scarf. 'Just like a knitting pattern - knit one, purl one, and with a blueprint like that, granny could knit a winter scarf that would stretch half way around the cosmos.' The audience took the joke.

'To embed a pattern, we slow the photons down to a halt, and capture a snapshot of their polarities, frozen in time. If the process in reversed, the information can be retrieved. Using single photon interference effects, it's possible to entangle pairs.'

Chris talked in depth for half an hour about nanotechnology. Erica listened intently. Much of the theory passed her by. However, she was captivated - captivated by his voice, by his manner, and captivated by his eyes. Every now and then, she felt him look at her and when he did, his eyes warmed her soul and enlivened her spirit.

'There is a race to be the first with the next generation of computers.' Chris continued, 'Whoever controls the next step, controls the future.' The slide changed to portray an oriental army of white coats in a laboratory.

'I would conclude by saying that we're only catching up with what Mother Nature has already invented. These are microtubules.' An image of noodle-like structures was projected. 'They form trackways for photons for the quantum computer inside our own head - our own brain.'

'Thank you all for paying attention and now, if you have any questions…' He looked around. 'The young man with the scarf again?'

'Just how big is a photon?'

'Good question. Let's look at the screen.'

The audience were expecting to view another image, but all they saw was white light.

'What you are looking at is something mysterious…' He pointed with a baton. 'Reflected light.' If this reflective surface is thinner than the size of the photon, some of the photons tunnel right through.' Walt Disney's Seven Dwarves came up on the screen. 'That's what we call quantum tunnelling… and here they are with their pick-axes, mining for crystals.'

Subdued laughter travelled around the auditorium.

'So you see, quantum mechanics is about real touchable stuff.'

Erica could tell that Chris was about to conclude his lecture. She tentatively raised her hand.

'Yes, the lady, next to the Professor.'

Why had she stood up? What was she going to ask him? For a few seconds she was silent. Then, she blurted out. 'Dr Credus, how long till we can send an email on a quantum computer?'

Laughter echoed around the auditorium.

Erica was embarrassed. What had made her ask such a naive question?

Chris shrugged his shoulders. 'Maybe it'll take ten years, maybe someone out there has already made one… and they are not letting on.'

Buoyed by his response, Erica felt confident enough to ask a further question. 'You mentioned pairs of entangled photons, how does that work?'

'This weird and wonderful world can get spooky. Non-locality is an amazing property - we would sure like to harness its power. Entangled photons can adopt the same polarization in an instant, as though through ESP.' Chris stared at directly at her. 'Photons can be invisibly entangled, keeping in touch, yet far apart. Like two lovers taken asunder.'

Erica felt her heart flip at his words.

Chris continued. 'If we could harness that, it would mean a force faster than light. Perhaps one day, in the not too distant future, magic and science will meet.'

The words left Erica enthralled.

'Thank you ladies and gentlemen. That concludes my talk on quantum computers. If you want to build one, blueprints are available… see me after.'

There was a round of amused chuckles.

'Seriously, we are a little sensitive about our specification, but if one of you has already put together a quantum computer in your garage,' he directed his question at the nervous young man with the scarf, 'let us know.'

Sunrise at Stonehenge appeared once more on the screen. 'I almost forgot,' Chris continued. 'You wanted to know the connection between the two? Einstein demonstrated the relationship between the three fundamental components of reality - energy, mass and light. His life long search was to find the secret code to unify all the forces in nature. Indeed, our ancient ancestors shared the same desire. Stonehenge is a reflection of that desire. Perhaps the quantum computer will be our Stonehenge. Perhaps at last, we are now on the threshold of discovering that unity. The quintessence, one might say.'

Erica leant over and whispered in Sam's ear. 'Where have I heard that word recently?'

Sam smiled.

The audience gave Dr Credus a standing ovation. He modestly acknowledged the applause and left the stage.

Chris took the passenger lift up to the laboratory.

Words of praise came from behind. 'Congratulations, that was a great talk.'

He turned around. 'Good to see you Sam, it's been a long time. Thanks for helping me out in the lecture.'

Sam made an introductory gesture towards Erica. 'Chris, this is Erica Janus.'

Chris's eyes sparkled. 'Those were great questions you asked, come into the unit both of you.' He ushered them through sliding doors into the glass-walled entrance lobby of the research unit, signed them passed security, and guided them into an office in the corner.

The young postgraduate, who had earlier been asking questions, hung up his scarf and Sam gave a knowing nod.

'A trick I learnt from you Sam, planting a few questions can help things go with a swing.' Chris made the introductions. 'My research assistant, Adrian, perhaps Sam and Mrs Janus would like to see our baby.'

Sam raised his eyebrows.

Adrian switched on the apparatus. An electronic hum filled the room. Two purple beams of laser light shone onto a central yellow crystal. 'These are photon strings.' Adrian began. 'Each photon in one beam has an entangled partner in the other. Inside the crystal,' he pointed to centre, 'each photon creates an interference pattern, like beads on a thread.'

Erica was mystified.

Adrian continued. 'The same pattern is recreated by its entangled partner. And the accumulation of these patterns forms a three-dimensional memory.'

'Pretty neat, isn't it...' completed Chris.

'Remarkable...' said Sam. 'You didn't say in your lecture you already had a quantum computer.'

'Something we reveal only on a need to know basis.' Chris winked at Erica.

She felt baffled.

'We're nearly there.' Chris walked the pair back to his desk and looked expectantly at them.

'We've brought something to show you.' Sam said. He turned to Erica.

She unbuckled the battered black holdall, placed the wooden box on the desk and gestured to Chris to open it.

The scientist unfolded the yellow cloth to uncover the crystal and held it to the light. 'Amazing.' His eyes flashed blue. 'Truly magnificent.' He was enthralled and shot a glance at Erica. 'I've never seen one quite like it. Where did you find it?'

'Near Witchbury, Dorset.' Erica said, sharing his excitement. 'Out on the Oakenland.'

'Fascinating.' Chris studied the stone.

Adrian joined them and picked up the crystal.

Chris continued. 'Adrian can run the crystal through the Electron Microscope and see how it shapes up. Sam, it's been at least a year since I enjoyed a pint of English beer, why don't we take Mrs Janus to lunch.'

She smiled. 'That would be lovely, do call me Erica. Don't forget it is only on loan, though. It's a birthday present for my daughter,' she explained.

'We'll take good care of it.' Chris assured her.

Adrian walked toward the microscope room and stared into the blue stone.

In the lift, Sam turned to Chris and asked, 'So, how are things?'

Chris was brusque. 'Not bad.'

Sam could tell that it was not the right moment to talk. When they were out of the building and walking along the street, Chris turned to Sam and was apologetic. 'It can be difficult in there. Things aren't quite the same as they were in your day.'

'I can see that,' Sam was impressed. 'It looks a pretty well lab equipped for a start.'

'We have the best computer research lab in the UK, and do you want to know why?' Chris paused.

Sam raised an eyebrow. 'Defence?'

Chris drew breath and looked around. 'It's discreet, but we're funded by the US government. Ultimately they own the kit and pay our wages - so naturally, they think they own our minds too.' There was a touch of cynicism in his voice.

Sam was philosophical. 'When you throw your hand in with the devil…'

Chris looked more serious. 'You know me, Sam; I don't like being dictated to - any more than you did twenty years ago. I'm from the old-school of academic independence, but I guess a billion a year means they have a right to see a return on their buck.'

'Sponsors…' Sam shrugged his shoulders. 'It's not new… even Leonardo da Vinci had that problem.'

'We may have advanced scientifically since his day,' Chris said doubtfully, 'but people are still motivated by greed and power.'

They entered the pub. Chris ordered drinks and sandwiches while Sam and Erica found a table. He joined them and continued. 'Science should be about sharing knowledge...' he paused. 'Take genetic engineering... it ought to be owned by us all, but it's the property of sharp-suited business men, savvy enough to patent the rights to the code.'

'But what can one do?' Erica sympathised. 'That's the way the world works nowadays.'

'Fundamental research should not belong to any one organisation. Knowledge belongs to all humanity,' insisted Chris.

Sam was sceptical. 'High ideals for such a commercial world.'

'If the sponsor finds out we are doing stuff that won't produce a quick enough return, they squash it, and who can blame them?'

Sam nodded. 'The Manhattan Project probably had the same misgivings.'

Chris looked serious. 'At least they knew what they were fighting for.' He looked quickly around the crowd in the pub. He continued in a quieter voice. 'Whoever finds the next paradigm in computing, can control everything.'

By the time they returned to the research centre, it was late afternoon. 'So what have we got?' asked Chris as he looked across at Adrian.

They noticed Adrian expression.

He seemed to be finding it difficult to control his composure. 'I couldn't believe it when I saw the results from the Electron Microscope. It's exactly what we've been looking for,' he continued, excitedly. 'It's a polymorph of GSQ.'

'Germanium silicon quartz,' Chris explained, at seeing Erica's puzzled expression.

'It has a unique, three-dimensional lattice.' Adrian scurried over to the computer on the desk and typed a password. Chris, Sam and Erica stood behind and looked at the image on the screen in amazement. A geometrical array of molecules rotated, until they reached one point on the screen when, like a key in a lock, they all perfectly aligned. The internal structure of the crystal had been revealed. Adrian pointed to an anomaly. 'Look you can even see where the fault line occurs - a thin layer of another material.'

'It's even better than the one they grew on Sky Lab,' Chris pulled down the privacy blind from the rest of the lab. 'Trying to grow germanium crystals in earth's gravity is a nightmare.'

'I'd love to see where you found this, Erica.' Chris looked at her expectantly.

'How about coming down to Dorset this weekend.' Sam suggested.

Erica's heart raced at the notion that Chris might come down to Dorset.

'I have a couple of spare days, before I go back to the States,' Chris explained. 'We'll leave the crystal with Adrian, and he can follow up the investigations.'

Erica felt electrified at the prospect but suddenly she was concerned. 'I don't really want to leave it.'

Chris pleaded 'This may be the breakthrough we've been looking for.' His eyes sparkled with excitement.

Erica found that look irresistible. 'You're not going to chop it up into pieces, are you?'

'The lab will be quiet over the weekend. Adrian can conduct tests using the photon laser. It won't come to any harm, it's just like keyhole surgery on a molecular scale.'

Something in his voice made her give in.

CHAPTER 18

The Journey Home

FRIDAY AFTERNOON THE LONDON train was crowded and it was impossible to talk. After crossing the capital, they discovered the Dorchester train packed too. After it had stopped at several suburban stations, there was at last, room for the three to sit together.

Sam leant forward toward Chris and was apologetic. 'My spare room is so full of junk. I hope you won't mind staying with my niece.'

'I'm looking forward to meeting Vicky, and treating myself to one of her proper English breakfasts.' Chris stretched out on the seat and relaxed.

'I'm still puzzled,' Erica said. 'I realise germanium quartz is uncommon, especially in a natural form... but what is it that puts the crystal in a totally different league?'

Chris turned toward Erica. 'There's a molecular mismatch between germanium and silicon. It results in a disruptive strain in the interfaces. The polymorph looks like a pure alloy and the lattices align perfectly. Tell me more about the place it was found.'

'My dog, Jet, discovered it. Then, he took it upon himself to go AWOL for two days. I thought he'd got trapped in one of the old workings.'

'It's a fascinating area, old silver mines mostly.' Sam explained. 'I've never come across germanium in Dorset though, could it have been man-made?'

Chris looked thoughtful. 'It would need intense heat and probably zero gravity.'

'Maybe it just fell out of the sky,' Erica joked.

They laughed.

Chris looked out of the carriage window at the greenness of the vegetation, so profuse and varied; he had dedicated his life to his work but, but over the last few months, he had started to realise he could never hope to achieve true peace of mind through work alone.

Sam and Chris continued to talk shop, but some distance into their journey, Sam began to flag. Chris and Erica smiled at each other as they watched him drift off to sleep. Sam began to snore lightly and Chris nodded towards him. 'We haven't met up for nearly twenty years, we've kept in touch on the net, though. Before university I grew up in this area… so it's an opportunity to return to old haunts.'

A flash crossed her mind. Had they met before? 'No wonder you know so much about the minerals here. What else can you tell me about the crystal? I'm dying to know everything. What did you say it was, a polymorph?'

'It's silicon that's undergone a change in its molecular pattern,' Chris explained.

'You mean like the difference between carbon and diamond?' Erica smiled when Chris look impressed and she nodded toward Sam. 'You and I have had the same teacher, don't forget.'

'We've already discovered your stone has some fascinating properties.' Chris continued. 'As I mentioned, we're looking for materials capable of capturing photons in entangled states.'

Intrigued, her mind went back to the question she had asked in the lecture theatre. 'Entangled states?' The words came out more sensually than she'd intended.

Chris stretched out his legs and leant back. 'How much do you know about quantum mechanics?'

'Only what I learnt at your lecture, and what Sam has taught me.' She gave him an amiable grin. 'I did try to read your article in the New Scientist, but it went a bit above my head.'

Chris studied her expression. 'Well, Einstein called it spooky action, at a distance. Two places at the same time.'

She looked puzzled. 'I knew science and magic are close, but can something be in two places at the same time?'

The announcement of their destination came over the public address.

'Looks like we don't have time right now.' Chris moved towards her. 'Why don't you and perhaps your husband come out to dinner tomorrow, and I could tell you more about entangled states.'

'I don't think Simon would be at all interested in quantum mechanics.' Erica looked at him with a blank expression.

'Your daughter, then?'

'Sarah will be away at her friend's.'

'How about an Italian?' Chris concluded.

'I don't know any Italians to invite.'

They laughed.

'No, that would be great,' she said. 'Italian food is my favourite.'

Sam stirred as the train slowed. 'Do excuse me, you two…' Sam rubbed his eyes and yawned. 'I do hope I wasn't snoring.'

Chris stood to retrieve his leather bag from the luggage rack. 'Sam, you have an instinct for waking up at the right time. Mrs Janus and I have a dinner date.'

Sam grinned. 'If we're going to spend the day looking at the geology, I'll be too whacked to join you.' They crossed the platform and walked toward Sam's car. 'But you're welcome to borrow my car.'

Chris looked Erica in the eye. 'Perfect,' he said.

CHAPTER 19

The Chocolate Tea Pot

CHRIS PULLED BACK THE curtains, opened the window wide, and took in a deep gulp of Dorset air. He had woken to a clear blue Spring sky. Why did Saturday still feel like the best day of the week? It must be a leftover from all the weekends spent as a child exploring the rock pools and cliff tops.

Before Chris had left the research unit, he had printed off geological maps of the area. He now unfolded them on the bed and oriented them to correspond with the view from the window. 'So... that must be the Hill...'

He could smell bacon. Breakfast called.

Chris had only met Vicky Fellows briefly on his arrival, the night before. She stood next to the coffee pot in the dining room and she welcomed him warmly. As she served up a full English breakfast, they chatted.

'Sam will be over in a few minutes,' he announced. 'We're spending the day on the Hill. Mrs Janus mentioned her dog went astray up there.'

Vicky nodded. 'Disappeared last weekend, on her birthday, too. God knows where... he just vanished, turned up two days later, though.'

'Labrador isn't he,' he confirmed. 'They're pretty good at finding their way home.'

'What are you hoping to discover, Doctor Credus?' Vicky asked. 'You're going to look where they found the crystal, I suppose.'

'Do you know the spot, Mrs Fellows?' Chris tucked into the breakfast and glanced over at Vicky.

'Couldn't say, exactly. Somewhere over on the east side, I think.' She poured him some coffee. 'All the mines were blocked off years ago. There are some weird shapes. It's often quite difficult to distinguish the Bronze Age earthworks from the mining spoil heaps, but Sam's got a good eye for these things. Do call me Vicky, by the way. It's valuable then, the crystal... must be, to bring you all this way?'

'It wasn't the only reason I came, Vicky.' He sipped his coffee. 'It's good to get the chance to come back. I spent my youth near here.'

Before she could ask more, there was a knock on the door. Sam greeted them. 'Morning...' He was in a buoyant mood. 'We'd better make an early start, the forecast's for rain.'

****

On Simon's phone, Beth was apologising. 'Simon, there was just a bit of a mix up over which photograph they were meant to use, that's all.'

The politician sat down at his study desk with a heavy grunt. 'It was a bloody disgrace!'

'You can't deny it achieved its objective we got the publicity.' Then, she simpered in a coquettish voice; 'Now Simon, how would you fancy dinner tonight in Dorchester...' she paused, waiting for a reaction. 'Maybe we could go somewhere after, you know, for a nightcap.'

Simon was a sucker for Beth's baby-doll tone. The thought of after dinner activity quelled Simon's irritation and the prospect of a meal out took appealed. 'We could go to the Italian... Luigi can sort out a discreet table.'

'That would be lovely,' Beth said. 'I'll leave you to book the room for later.'

Erica stood at the door of the study. Simon smiled benignly and slid into business mode. 'I'll pick you up at seven.' He slipped the phone into his pocket.

Erica was matter of fact. 'I came to tell you Dr Credus has invited me for a meal, tonight.'

'Oh that's ok, I'll be out anyway.' Simon said, stiffly. 'My agent, needs to talk.'

Erica looked reassured. 'About that appalling photo, no doubt.' She shut the door and felt a tangible sense of relief.

****

Vicky and Erica made their way to the remaining vacant table at the window of the Chocolate Tea Pot café.

The waitress came over to them and Vicky ordered two cappuccinos.

Erica looked concerned as she recognised the purple braids. 'Dee, how are you?' she asked, 'Your mother said you'd been ill.'

The waitress took down the order and stifled a reply. 'All right now, thanks.' She then cut short further talk and disappeared back to the kitchen.

Erica leant over to Vicky. 'Beebee said her daughter had food poisoning.' I wonder why she dashed off?'

Vicky looked puzzled. 'She seemed too embarrassed to talk about it.' Then, she added in a whisper, 'Hope it wasn't drugs.'

Erica became anxious. 'Dee and Sarah are classmates.'

'I'm sure she's fine.' Vicky tried to reassure her and moved the conversation on. 'Was your daughter upset at not getting the crystal back?'

Erica sipped her coffee, 'I haven't told her yet.' She paused to judge Vicky's reaction before imparting her news. 'Dr Credus has invited me out for an Italian meal tonight.' Then she added, 'He invited Sarah too, but she's at her friend's again this weekend.'

Vicky looked at her with a hint of envy. 'He's not my type,' she teased and added in a quiet tone, 'I suppose Dr Credus is quite handsome in a boyish sort of way.'

Erica looked at her askance. 'There's nothing like that going on.' Her denial was louder than she intended and she became suddenly aware of the others in the coffee shop. A couple in walking gear sat in one corner, and three young girls sat together in another. She thought the teenagers looked familiar. Near the door were two men in dark suits. They exchanged looks with Erica and Vicky.

Vicky changed the subject. 'I can't see this weather lasting, can you? I'm sure it's going to break soon.'

As Vicky and Erica rose to leave, they noticed that the men's city shoes were covered in mud. One of the men stood, and smiled to expose a gold tooth. He opened the door for them. Vicky nodded an acknowledgement.

They had walked only a short distance, when Erica turned to Vicky. 'Am I getting paranoid? Those two in the café - they were as alien as if they'd just disembarked from a spaceship.'

Vicky nodded. 'Did you notice their shoes?' There was a clap of thunder and large spots began to fall 'Oh no, not again,' she yelped, and they hurried to their cars. 'Enjoy yourself tonight, Erica.'

CHAPTER 20

The Restaurant

THE PARADISO WAS FULLY booked. The headwaiter took Beth's coat. '*Grazie* Luigi.' Simon said in a superior tone.

Luigi winked at Beth as he touched the side of his nose with a forefinger. 'Now you're so famous Mr Janus, we have a special table.'

They were ushered to the back of the restaurant. When seated, Simon nervously glanced around the restaurant. 'Bloody hell!' He turned immediately to Beth and shuffled his seat to hide behind a large potted plant.

Beth looked at him, quizzically.

'This scientist chap,' Simon stuttered. 'What do you know about him?'

'I looked him up on the net. There was a photo.' Beth threw Simon a pained expression.

'By the window in the green dress,' he said, agitated.

Beth turned her head to peer across to the other side of the room. She caught sight of a couple. The man in the open neck shirt and crisp grey flannels, she recognised immediately. 'That's him, that Credus! Don't tell me, that lady with him – that's your wife.' Beth turned around for a better look and stared across at them.

Simon bristled. 'I didn't know they were coming here,' he said in a tense whisper.

'Evidently.' Beth's reply was dispassionate.

'I think we'd better go…' Simon mopped his brow with a napkin. 'We could nip out the back.'

'No way! What's wrong with you.' Beth became annoyed. 'We're having a meal. There's no harm. I wouldn't mind getting an interview sorted with that scientist. He's quite a dish. I might just go over and say hi. He looks quite cool.'

'For God's sake, be serious.' Simon looked uneasy. 'I'm not supposed to be here.' He continued to keep his head down. 'You haven't got a thing for him, have you?' Simon asked petulantly.

'You're paranoid, Simon.' Beth was incensed. 'Give Luigi a bigger tip next time and we can be shepherded into the broom cupboard.' She pouted her lips and changed to a sultry tone. 'Now, have you booked a room?'

'The Green Man,' he whispered, tetchily. 'I got a good reduction from Jerry. Being an MP has some perks, after all.'

Beth rolled her eyes. 'Cheapskate,' she muttered under her breath.

****

'Did your husband mind?' Chris asked.

'He has a dinner appointment. I'm quite relieved, actually. Things are a bit fraught between us.' Erica glanced at Chris's face to judge his reaction. 'We lead separate lives… Well almost,' she added.

Chris briefly touched her arm. 'It happens.' He passed over the menu to her and she stared at the long list of Italian dishes. Chris sensed Erica was having difficulty making up her mind. 'I'll start with Linguini Primavera,' he suggested.

'Primavera…' Erica whispered.

'It's pasta with a Spring vegetables,' he explained.

Erica paused. 'I'll have the same…' She hesitated again and looked into the distance. 'It just brought something to mind.'

'Let me guess,' Chris grinned and shot her a look, 'it reminds you of Botticelli.'

Erica tried hard not to stare into his eyes, but ripples of anticipation shot down her spine.

'I have to confess,' he said in a relaxed tone, 'I gleaned that snippet from Sam.'

'Ah, in the Emporium, yes, it is one of my favourite paintings,' she smiled. They ordered their meal. The waiter poured out a bottle of Chianti with a flourish.

Chris raised his glass. 'To the crystal...' He looked earnestly at her. 'I hope you didn't mind that we kept it for further tests.'

'It's my daughter who'll be upset. I haven't told her. She's away tonight at friends.'

'Perhaps you'll let me take you both out, for lunch tomorrow. We could go to the Green Man. I had beer and sandwiches there with Sam earlier. They have a real log fire. We needed it to dry out.'

She smiled as the waiter brought their starter. 'That would be lovely.' It would provide a further chance to see him before he went back.

Sam and I had a good time looking at the ancient structures, and the old silver-mine workings,' Chris continued, 'but we got carried away exploring, and then got soaked.'

'I can sometimes be up there with Jet for hours without realizing...' Erica's voice had become rather dreamy. 'If you get chance to visit the church there's a stained-glass window showing miners in leather caps from the Middle Ages,' Erica suggested. 'You seem quite at home here already.'

'I must confess, I do feel a certain pull here,' Chris admitted. 'If I feel like this tomorrow, I'll not want to get back on the plane on Monday.'

Erica looked at him, earnestly. 'You're not serious.'

'It's true...' Chris said. 'It's still my home in a way.'

'You were about to tell me on the train. I thought your accent had a familiar ring,' Erica looked at him, quizzically.

'Quite correct Miss Marple, I lived in Dorset for a while, in my teens.'

'So being in Dorset *is* almost like coming home for you. Now I also understand why you know so much about the minerals around here.'

The waiter brought the main course.

Chris refilled their glasses. 'I've always enjoyed fossil collecting, long before I became involved with quantum physics.'

She smiled into his eyes. Briefly, she lost herself. 'Ah yes you were going to tell me more about entangled pairs.'

'A digital computer uses switches, in two states - yes and no. A quantum computer uses three,' Chris explained in a self-assured tone.

'Yes, no and maybe?' Erica joked. 'It must have even more problems making up its mind about the menu than I do.'

'Strange you should say that in some ways quantum computers are like the human mind. For instance, we are investigating entangled photons...' Chris glanced into her eyes, 'it's possible the human brain uses them too.'

'The wine's wonderful.' Erica wondered if the Chianti was putting her into a quantum state. She recalled the lecture. 'I know what a photon is...' She noticed the flame from the candle reflected in his eyes, '...a particle of light.'

'Absolutely.' Chris continued. 'There's an unseen force that exists throughout the universe. If we can begin to understand how it works, it might be the key to the next step.'

'The next step?' She leaned towards him. 'An unseen force?' Erica repeated. Her mind became alive to numerous possibilities the words offered. 'And as far as the crystal is concerned?'

'We need your help, Erica.' He looked at her, pleadingly. 'If it was formed out on the Oakenland, perhaps there are others.'

Her eyes glazed over as she stared into the reflections in her wine glass. The two candles on the dining table turned into two fires - the flames lit up the faces of Wyllow and the Hendasfolk.

'Why the far-away look?' asked Chris.

'The Oakenland… it's so ancient. It's a special place,' she stated and her heart suddenly dipped. 'I wouldn't want to see it ruined by people excavating for minerals.'

'I should think your stone is a one-off,' Chris tried to reassure her. 'But to be absolutely sure, we would need to carry out further tests in the area it was found, but they wouldn't be disruptive.'

Have you told anyone else? What about your research unit?'

'Sam mentioned your love for the landscape, but if we don't investigate the site, someone else might get in there first.'

'Not if we don't tell them.' Erica pleaded.

'It was weird but,' Chris looked at her with a frown, 'we came across a couple of guys out on the Hill this morning, they were dressed in city suits.'

Erica was concerned. 'I think I saw them this morning in the café.'

'For the time being, I agree,' said Chris, 'it's best to keep quiet. The cat could easily get out the bag.'

'That wouldn't be Shrödinger's Cat, would it?' Erica tried to make light of it.

Chris chuckled, 'Sam's been instructing you in quantum physics after all.'

Erica expression suddenly changed. She had caught sight of the young reporter and realised the man behind the pot plant was her husband.

'What's up?' Chris asked and looked over in the direction of her gaze.

Erica glanced nervously around. She did not want them spoiling her evening. 'Nothing, I'm sorry.' She tried to regain her composure. 'It's just the idea that there might be geophysicists crawling all over the area.'

Chris continued, 'I wouldn't worry, we can forget about that for a while.' He poured out the remaining wine into her glass.

She looked thoughtful. 'Anyway it's owned by the Church. They wouldn't let anything happen to it. The area's part of our heritage and far too beautiful to change.'

When coffee arrived, she glanced over to Simon's table. It was now empty. 'I'm sorry if I seemed preoccupied, my husband was sitting over there.'

'He should have joined us,' Chris replied.

'He was with a woman,' Erica stated in a deadpan voice, 'a reporter I think.'

'Business or pleasure?' Chris enquired.

'It didn't look like business,' Erica said flatly.

When they left a few minutes later, it was raining. Neither had brought umbrellas and for a few seconds they stood under the canopy of the restaurant.

'I'll get the car,' Chris said. 'Wait here.'

'It's only rain…' Erica was not going to wait alone and they began to walk down the road.

He removed his jacket, placed it over their heads and took her hand. Coming out from the warm restaurant into the cool wet night air, made them gasp. They half ran down the dimly lit street. When they arrived at the car, they were soaked through. Chris opened the driver's door of Sam's Volvo and ushered Erica in.

'I thought you were driving,' she asked. Erica found it endearing that someone so intelligent could forget which side the driver sat.

'I had a quantum leap back to the States,' Chris joked. They sat in the car. Erica felt the wetness against her skin and shivered, yet she did not want the evening to end.

'It was my turn to be distracted.' He looked at her body through the rain soaked dress.

Chris reached over to the back seat and retrieved a travel rug. 'Throw this around you. I hope I didn't bore you with all that shop talk?'

'Quite the contrary, it made a change to be able to discuss such things, it was fascinating.'

She touched her neck and she suddenly looked sad.

'Are you ok?' Chris looked at her, intently.

'I've lost something I've always treasured. Someone gave it to me a long time ago. I wanted to show it to you. It was an ammonite. Never mind.'

'Sorry to hear that.' Chris was sympathetic but inwardly he smiled to himself. Erica had just confirmed something that he already knew, but he would wait for the right moment before he told her. He started the car and they set off back along the unlit country roads.

Every now and then, they had to slow down in order for Erica to give directions. She looked out into the darkness. They came to a signpost. 'Wait, this isn't the way back to Melbury.

Chris had suddenly taken a left fork. He turned to her. 'We're not going to Melbury,' he said emphatically. 'We're going to Witchbury.' He reached over and gently touched her hand and added, 'The Green Man has a log fire.'

CHAPTER 21

The Green Man

THE GREEN MAN HAD grown haphazardly over the centuries to meet the demands of the times. In the Middle Ages, its role had been assured by the bringing together of three cottages to form a drinking parlour. As a coaching Inn in the eighteenth century, an additional wing had provided overnight lodgings. In modern times, its shambling muddle now not only provided the archetypal village pub, but also the ideal backdrop for a romantic hideaway.

The girl with purple-braids was sitting behind the reception desk. This was Dee's second Saturday job. She yawned and looked forward to midnight at the end of a long day. As she awaited the late arrivals, she doodled on the pad of hotel writing paper - a cross within a diamond. At half past eleven, Simon stumbled through the door.

'I've a room...' he whispered, 'name of Janus.'

'Good evening, Mr Janus - you're famous.' She handed him a key. 'Sign here for room 4, it's our best room.'

Simon looked sheepish, scribbled an illegible flourish and proceeded up to the room.

As instructed, two minutes later, Beth entered the hotel through the Snug and snuck up the back stairs. Simon glanced up and down the corridor as he held open the door to the room.

'Why don't you sort out a bottle of bubbly while I have a shower,' Beth proposed.

Simon reached for the phone. 'I'll give Jerry a tinkle.'

****

Chris and Erica arrived just before midnight. Their clothes were still damp from the rain and they laughed as they snuggled close to the log fire.

'It's late. You could stay here tonight, I'm sure Vicky won't mind.' Erica suggested. 'I can take a taxi back.'

'That's not a bad idea, at least the first part. I'll see if they have a room. Come up and find me in five minutes and we'll say goodnight.' Chris left Erica in the bar, and entered reception.

Dee smiled at him. 'We only have a double left. Number 3, sign here.' She handed him the key. He continued up to the room.

Erica entered reception two minutes later. She was taken aback to see Dee.

'Hello again Mrs Janus,' Dee looked at her expectantly. 'Your husband's in Room 4; romantic night for two?'

Erica acknowledged her with an uneasy smile, nodded and continued up the stairs without a word.

Chris was waiting outside Room 3.

Disorientated, Erica eyed with suspicion the Champagne tray in front of Room 4. 'Did you say I was your wife?'

'No,' Chris looked mystified, 'but what a lovely idea.'

****

Dee handed Will the key to Room 5. 'You've got the last unoccupied room. Don't make too much noise, I'll lose my job if Jerry finds out you haven't paid.'

'Don't worry,' Will replied, 'I'll make sure we don't get caught.' Will called to his friend and they tiptoed up the back stairs and crept around the tray of Bollinger and two glasses outside Room 4.

****

A minute later, Simon poked out his head, glanced furtively up and down the corridor and dragged the tray into Room 4. Beth was dressed in a French Maid outfit. He put the bottle on the table, took a flying leap onto the bed, and let out a primeval, heehawwheehaww...

****

In Room 5, the blonde girl sat bolt upright. 'Good grief...'

'What's up?' Will asked.

'...That sounded just like my dad!'

'Don't be silly,' Will said sardonically, 'it's just guilty paranoia.'

****

In Room 3, Erica stiffened.

'What is it?' Chris asked.

She listened for a few seconds. 'Nothing...' she chose to dismiss the noise as an unaccountable acoustic aberration and relaxed back into the sensual embrace.

****

Erica awoke in the grey light of dawn, slid out of bed and gathered her clothes from the floor. As she dressed, Chris stirred. She leant over and gave him a kiss on the brow. 'I'm going to have to get back before everyone wakes up.' She whispered, and headed for the door.

'I'll speak to you later...' Chris blew her a kiss and drifted off back to sleep with a contented sigh.

What had she done? She filled with guilt. Erica descended the stairs. In front of her, a shock of blond hair bobbed down the flight and disappeared into the reception area. 'Wyllow?' she called out in a whisper. When she arrived in reception, it was empty.

CHAPTER 22

The Interview

FROM ERICA'S BEDROOM WINDOW the early morning sun was a greyed-out circle. Like the misty veil hanging over the Oakenland, her mind was shrouded - what should she do about her marriage... the crystal... Chris...

Erica had walked back in the early hours from the Green Man, and Jet had greeted her like a long lost friend. There was no sign of Simon and she found herself feeling relieved. If her marriage were a sham, why not admit the hypocrisy of it all, have it out in the open, and do something about it? But in the morning light, things had changed. The crystal now seemed to have put the woodland under threat and put her relationship with Chris at risk. What sort of relationship did she have anyway... had it been just a one-night-stand? After all, he would be leaving for the States the following morning.

When he phoned her, she would ask Chris to return the crystal.

****

Chris tried to ring Erica, but from his mobile, the signal was too erratic. He drove back to the Four Winds in Sam's Volvo. When he arrived, Vicky was waiting with breakfast. 'Sorry the bacon's frazzled.'

Chris detected some stiffness in her voice. 'No problem.'

'Did you have a good time last night?' Vicky quizzed.

'It was a great meal.'

There was a silence. Chris knew she was waiting for an explanation of why he hadn't spent the night at Four Winds.

'So what's on the menu today?' Vicky asked, but the phone rang before he could answer her. 'Dr Credus, it's for you, someone called Beth Frank.'

Chris thanked her. 'I could see you for lunch… yes fine… twelve thirty, the Green Man.' Chris put down the receiver. A second later he cursed. Last night he had suggested Sunday lunch with Erica.

Vicky noisily cleared away the dishes and Chris retreated to his room to ring Erica. 'Hi, I've been trying to get hold of you… I'm at Four Winds, I just wanted to say about last night… it was wonderful. I should have given you a lift back but I was whacked. It must have been jet lag catching up.' He missed her reply. 'Sorry the signal's breaking up… I really want to see you again for lunch but my day is full, and I'm off back to Cambridge this afternoon. I'll phone again later.'

****

Simon was surprised to come across his daughter walking home from Witchbury so early. He pulled up. She climbed into the passenger seat. 'Thanks Dad… did you and mum have a good time last night?'

He was taken aback. 'The meal was fine,' he stuttered. How about your sleepover?'

She ignored his question. 'Where's mum?'

'At home, I expect.' Simon looked puzzled, 'Why?'

Again, she ignored her father. When they arrived Erica was in the lounge, talking on her mobile. 'I'll come over…' She did not complete her sentence.

Sarah jumped in immediately, 'Who was that?'

'A scientist, he's carrying out some experiments on the crystal.' Erica felt she didn't want to say more.

'Mum, you told me you wouldn't let the crystal go.' Sarah was distraught. 'When are they going to give it back?'

'In a couple of days.' Erica looked bewildered. 'How was your sleepover?'

Sarah frowned. 'I don't do sleepovers, but how was yours?' Sarah left for her room without waiting for a reply.

'Teenagers huh...' Simon quipped and sat down to read the Sunday paper. 'I don't know where she was last night, but I picked her up about a mile outside Witchbury.'

Erica felt uneasy at her daughter's reaction, but her retreat had provided a way out before further questions dragged Erica in any deeper. 'I'll have a word with her, later. Come on Jet.' She rattled his lead. 'I'm going over to see Vicky. I'll be out for lunch. You haven't forgotten the tea party at three at the Manse have you...'

Simon continued to read the paper without looking up. 'I'll be there.'

****

Chris had laid out his maps on the bed. There was a knock on the door. He opened it.

'Hi, I'm Will.'

'Of course...Vicky's son.' Chris welcomed him in.

Will cast his eye over the maps, 'Geological,' he stated, 'so what are you interested in finding?'

The intensity in Will's voice took Chris aback. 'Your mother may have mentioned...' Chris began calmly, 'I'm investigating a crystal Mrs Janus found.' He wanted to engage Will and so he pointed to the Cauldron field and asked, 'There seems to be an odd anomaly here, do you know what it could be?'

Will took no notice and continued, 'You don't know how special it is.'

'The stone, you mean.' Chris wanted to allay his fears. 'It's potentially of great scientific interest.'

'Return it...' Will insisted. 'It doesn't belong to you.'

'It belongs to Mrs Janus.' Chris remained composed. 'She wanted us to see what we can find out about it.'

Will pulled Chris around to face him and stared the scientist in the eye. 'Bring it back...' he cried. He turned, strode out and slammed the door.

Chris muttered to himself, 'What the hell was that all about?'

When shortly before twelve, there was a quiet knock on the door, Chris half expected it to be Will returning to apologise. It was Erica.

She spoke, hurriedly. 'My phone cut out. I wanted to see you about lunch.'

He embraced her and handed her a bunch of flowers he had bought at the hotel. 'I'm so sorry. I've got to meet up with someone on business. I'll ring you before I leave.'

'Thanks...' She looked at him quizzically. 'For the flowers, I mean,' she added.

Chris brought his bags downstairs and loaded them into Sam's car. He wound down the window and gave Erica a smile.

She managed to return a wave and watched him slowly drive away. When the car had gone, she glanced across to Vicky. Erica felt lost.

****

In a low cut black cocktail dress, and wearing a diamante necklace, Beth was relaxing on a sofa in the lounge bar. She sipped a Martini.

Chris strode into the bar. 'Sorry I'm a little late, I had to take Sam's car back. He's not feeling up to driving, so I'll need to get a taxi to Dorchester for the London train, after lunch.'

'I'll give you a lift, it's on my way,' Beth offered.

Ten minutes later, they were at the window table in the restaurant. 'The article is for the women's section of a national Sunday.'

Chris's mobile rang, and he took it from his pocket and switched it off. He smiled at the journalist, apologetically.

Beth sipped her drink and moved her chair closer to his.

****

Erica put her mobile back under the dashboard. She had parked at the Green Man. She could see them at the lunch table. She even saw him take out his phone. How ridiculous to think that last night had meant anything. How naïve… how old-fashioned… but then, after all, they had only just met, hadn't they? Marriage was boring, but at least it was safe. Today she was forty, yet emotionally she was seventeen.

A whole hour passed. As they left, Erica watched as Chris ease into the bucket seat in Beth's sports car, and stared in tearful disbelief as the red blur drove out of sight.

So, Vicky was right.

CHAPTER 23

The Tea Party

THE MANSE, A VICTORIAN gothic pile, stood alone some hundred yards from the church, behind a dense thicket of conifers and shrubs. The gravel crunched under the wheels of the VW as Erica drew up next to Vicky's Morris. She waited a few seconds to compose herself.

After witnessing Beth and Chris, she had gone to see Sam. He had been supportive, but she was still feeling upset. She took a deep breath and headed for the front door. An old BSA motorbike stood propped up against the porch.

Erica tugged the bell pull. An echo from the hallway made a satisfying distant clang. After a few seconds, Erica heard the clipped approach of a woman's footsteps. The door opened to reveal the diminutive housekeeper, neatly attired in a grey pinafore dress and white blouse.

'Mrs Janus,' the housekeeper said, stiffly. 'Your husband's been here some time.'

'I'm a little late.' Erica apologised. 'Miss Tweedy isn't it?'

'This way - follow me.' She led Erica along an imposing tiled hall, through an anteroom, and then into the lounge.

Erica stared around her. An elaborate frieze of cupids and angels bordered the high ceiling. Strewn like desert islands on a sea of bare floorboards, wear-worn Persian carpets defined the territory of the groups gathered in the capacious room. The guests chatted amongst themselves in twos and threes. She caught sight of Vicky and Simon. They were sitting in a corner of one of the ornate bay windows on a sun-faded sofa. Kneebone was dressed in dark grey, and held a tray of canapés. He stood motionless in front of the drinks cabinet, at seeing Erica, he gave a smirk, and shuffled toward her.

The Reverend Radpole immediately disengaged himself from three middle-aged women and intercepted him. 'Mrs Janus, hello again my dear, welcome to our vicarage.'

'I'm sorry I'm a little late.' Erica was conscious her voice sounded strained and she tried to relax. 'It's so grand, I'd no idea it would be so decorative inside.' She gazed around at the ornamentation.

'I always say it reflects my character rather well.' The Reverend chuckled. 'A touch dour on the outside, but a treasure deep within - takes a good deal of looking after, of course. Maintenance costs are very high. My housekeeper and Dodo,' he nodded in their direction, with a hint of resignation.

'Quite a responsibility, along with the church, too.' Erica agreed.

'We do our best but I'm not sure for how much longer we can keep going. The Commissioners have threatened to close St Michael's and sell off the Manse as a hostel for asylum seekers. They threatened to turf me out, to some pokey flat up country.'

'How dreadful.' Erica was alarmed.

'Your dear husband has a plan, but I'm sworn to secrecy. Anyway, I understand that celebrations are in order.' A playful smile flashed across Radpole's face. 'Your stray turned up.'

Erica threw a glance at Simon, 'He came back of his own accord, this morning.'

Simon stood up and sprang over toward them. Beebee, Miss Tweedy and Vicky joined them, closely followed by Kneebone with the tray of canapés. He stood in silence behind Beebee. Erica suspected he had come over to snoop.

'Rodney,' Simon scoffed in an ebullient mood. 'Did my clever wife tell you she discovered a crystal?'

Erica projected an indignant stare at her husband.

The Reverend took a step closer to Erica. 'No, do tell more, Mrs Janus, it sounds fascinating.'

Vicky chipped in. 'It's beautiful... it's almost the size of your fist, Rodney.'

'How wonderful,' the Reverend exclaimed. 'Where was it found?'

'On the Oakenland,' Vicky proclaimed, enthusiastically.

Erica glared at Vicky, but it was too late. She knew why Radpole had asked - the Church owned most of the land. Of all people to start to talk about the crystal, she had not expected it of Vicky. The damage done, the conversation moved up another gear.

Simon was full of himself. 'Have you had any other finds round here, Rodney?'

'None that I know of,' Radpole looked intrigued, 'but precious stones are discovered in mines, aren't they.'

'Apparently, it's very special.' Vicky interjected. 'Chris Credus, one of Sam's post-graduates from his Cambridge days over from the States is looking into it.' Vicky continued, 'He's been staying at Four Winds.'

Erica glowered at Vicky. Under the influence of a couple of cheap sherries and in the presence of men, Vicky had become another person, and broadcast all Erica's secrets. Why not preach it from the pulpit, for God's sake! She felt powerless - let down by Chris, and now betrayed by her best friend.

'You look troubled, my dear.' Radpole noticed Erica's expression.

'It's just...' Erica was dumbstruck but managed to put a few words together. 'It's just we wouldn't want hundreds of treasure seekers digging up the Oakenland.'

'I hardly think Witchbury will turn into the Klondike.' Radpole chuckled, glibly. 'No need to worry.'

Everyone laughed at his remark. Erica remained stoical.

'Of course,' he continued in a more serious tone, 'the Church Commissioners will have to be informed, it could be of archaeological interest.'

Uneasy at seeing Erica's reaction, Vicky began to realize what she had done. 'Don't be silly Rodney,' she retorted, 'surely, there's such a thing as treasure trove?'

The Reverend pondered. 'If the find's of any value, it could help with church funds.'

Simon re-entered into the conversation. 'Rodney... what an excellent idea.'

Erica could not believe it. They were all talking as though the crystal were now common property. The subject moved on to raising funds for the church roof by imposing a chancel tax, and then to the state of the village cricket pavilion.

Simon looked at his watch. 'Sorry folks, I have to leave. Vicky's offered me a lift to the station.'

'I have to go into Dorchester on an errand.' Vicky was quick to explain.

Erica gave her an enquiring look. She seemed oblivious to any sense of disapproval. 'You haven't had too many sherries have you, Vicky?'

'Only two glasses,' she chirruped.

She and Simon left the room escorted by Miss Tweedy.

Erica was determined to try to set things straight with the Reverend. 'Rodney, could I ask you not to mention the crystal, at least, not until we know if it's of any value?'

Radpole sidled up close to her and placed his hand on her wrist. 'I understand your concern... softly, softly eh? So, when will we know if it's valuable?'

'In a few weeks, I should think.' Erica reasoned that if she could create some breathing space, interest in the crystal might die down. She tried to sound dismissive. 'Sam didn't think it was that valuable.'

'Of course,' Radpole grimaced, 'it's not always the monetary worth of something that makes it precious.' He patted Erica on the wrist.

Beebee seemed to want to be friendly. 'Hello Erica, did you find out all you wanted from Rodney's pamphlet?'

It was becoming obvious she could not expect to keep anything to herself in Witchbury. Erica felt besieged.

The Reverend's face beamed. 'Oh my dear, you didn't tell me you were interested in the Lady in White. I became interested in her not long after I first moved here. Miss Tweedy put me on to it.' Rodney gave her a benign look.

Miss Tweedy looked apprehensive.

'Have you seen the ghost, Miss Tweedy?' Beebee asked.

'There are some things,' Miss Tweedy replied, nervously, 'best kept to oneself.'

Radpole stepped in. 'So, Mrs Janus, did you agree with my theory?'

Beebee gave the Reverend an admiring look. 'I'm positive you're right Rodney, it must be St Catherine, you're such a scholar.'

'It could be,' Erica said, with an air of the sceptic, 'but Sam said that the name cader ryn means hill throne in Celtic.'

'I was only putting forward one hypothesis. Perhaps you have a theory of you own, Mrs Janus?'

Before she could respond, the doorbell rang, Miss Tweedy scurried off and Beebee looked out of the window to see who had arrived. 'Who on earth is that, now…'

Erica was about to mention the Celtic priestess, when Beebee whispered in her ear, 'Did you have a good time last night? My daughter, told me you and your husband were in the Green Man - how Romantic.'

Erica looked perplexed and whispered to Beebee, 'I think she must have been confused.'

Miss Tweedy returned followed by someone Erica was not expecting to see again that day. What was *she* doing here? The girl with copper hair was wearing the same revealing black cocktail dress and diamante necklace that Erica had witnessed earlier.

'Hello everyone, I'm Beth Frank.'

'You're very welcome,' the Reverend smiled. He took two paces over toward her. 'What brings you to our little party?'

'Mr Janus mentioned you were having a get-together. I was over in this neck of the woods and I thought I might drop in.'

'You've just missed Mr Janus,' the Reverend ushered her into the group by putting a hand on her shoulder. 'But do join us.'

Erica eyed Beth suspiciously. Not two hours before, Erica had witnessed her drive off with Dr Credus, and now she was back. Was she a spy - if so, for whom, Simon or Chris?

Beth looked at the vicar with a serious expression. 'As a reporter, it helps to get on intimate terms with village life.'

'You've come to the right place, Miss Frank,' Radpole gushed over her, 'we're very friendly here.'

Kneebone smirked.

'So I've discovered.' Beth extended her hand toward Erica, 'Hello Mrs Janus, we haven't met.'

'No we haven't, but I think you know my husband.' Erica was not sure how long she could torture herself by being in the same room as the journalist. 'I gather that you were the person responsible for Simon hitting the front page of the tabloids.'

Beth was unabashed. 'George, the editor, put a veto on it; *the Echo* didn't want to upset the local custom,' the reporter explained. 'I got in contact with a colleague in Docklands. Mr Janus was all for going global.'

'He went global all right, when he saw the front page,' Erica exclaimed, 'if not stratospheric.'

Beth returned a calm smile. 'He certainly seems to back on terra firma again now and, all is forgiven. There was just a mix up over the right photo.'

'They say all publicity's good publicity,' Radpole pontificated.

'Talking about publicity Mrs Janus,' Beth continued, 'I've just been talking to Dr Credus. He was fascinating. He mentioned you'd found... a crystal.'

'Erica has discovered a stunning one,' the Reverend, interjected. 'Everyone wants to see it. It sounds wonderful. It's just the sort of story your readers would be fascinated in reading, I'm sure,' the Reverend declared.

Beth looked at Erica with a probing expression. 'Do tell me more, Mrs Janus.'

Erica felt sick. How could Chris have told Beth, about the crystal? What had he told Beth? Erica could see what the journalist was up to. She was obviously a clever and ambitious. Erica was struck dumb.

'Perhaps you might bear me in mind, when you feel you have a story to tell, Mrs Janus? Do have my card.'

Erica thanked Beth, weakly, and dropped it in her bag.

Kneebone sidled up to Beth with the sweet tray. 'Meringue?' he growled. His voice was deeper than Erica expected.

'Mmm... they do look scrummy, I may have one later.' The tray began to judder, precariously. Beth took a sudden side step away from Kneebone.

The Reverend chipped in again. 'I hope you're not finding this area too boring, Miss Frank?'

'On the contrary Reverend, after London I imagined it might be difficult to find stories, but things seem to keep falling into my lap.' She threw another glance at Erica.

Beebee let out a loud exclamation. 'Ewwww!' She turned around to see Kneebone wink at her and she flushed red.

Radpole turned to Beebee. 'Was it the Mexican dip?'

Beebee looked uncomfortable. 'Is that what you call it!'

Miss Tweedy chirped up and addressed Beth. 'I would have thought there was nothing down here to interest a young woman from the city.'

'It's often the small things that have the most impact.' Beth swung her handbag over her shoulder. It hit Kneebone squarely on the jaw. The tray flew out his hands. Powdered sugar exploded over Miss Tweedy.

Radpole glanced apprehensively toward the drinks cabinet. The level of the whisky in the decanter had receded. He looked around for Kneebone. He had disappeared.

'I'm terribly sorry,' Beth stooped to pick up the meringues. From the rear of her skirt, she brushed off telltale icing-sugar fingerprints. 'He received his just dessert, I think,' she declared under her breath.

CHAPTER 24

The Proposition

THE LONDON TRAIN PULLED slowly away from Dorchester. Chris looked along the aisle and recognised Erica's husband in the next compartment. He dialled her number and left a message. 'I just wanted to say last night was wonderful. Sorry I couldn't stay longer. I should be back in about three weeks, and would love to see you again.' He settled down behind the foil of the broadsheet and perused the business section. A few minutes later, the scientist's phone rang. It was Adrian and he was excited. The news from the lab was that the crystal was providing some amazing results. 'That's great,' said Chris. 'I'll meet you at the lab about nine, tonight, as soon as I arrive. I'm flying back early tomorrow.'

Chris relaxed and watched the scenery roll by as the train made its way through soft green downland pastures. He turned his attention to Simon. In the next compartment, two men had sat down and shaken hands with the MP. They looked familiar. He remembered he had seen them the previous morning, near the Portal Stone. He watched as they spread out a drawing in front of them and marked out an area in red.

Chris decided he would pay a visit to the buffet. As he walked passed the group, Chris glanced at the document on the table.

Simon glanced up and immediately he covered the plan with his briefcase. They exchanged a brief nod. Chris had recognised it instantly. It was a map of the Oakenland.

****

Erica had returned home dejected. She was disappointed about Vicky, downhearted about Chris, annoyed at Beth, and worried about the crystal.

She took solace by logging on to the net on the new laptop. Once more, the password '34125' came up automatically. On the screen, a name appeared that set her heart beating - Wyllow. Through the magic of technology, someone was there she could talk to. She found herself unable to stop the words that flowed through her fingers. He seemed to appreciate, to know… to have a genuine understanding. How was it that he was so perceptive? Within an hour, she had told him about the events at the tea party, her fears and uncertainties about her relationships, the crystal in Cambridge, and the threat to the Oakenland.

Her respondent ended with one sentence…'Don't worry… … the Icera Stone will be returned to its rightful place.'

'Wyllow, before you go,' Erica typed, 'does 34125 mean anything to you?'

'ERICA 34125 ICERA. It's as simple as ABC.'

CHAPTER 25

The Primavera

ERICA FELT RESTLESS. HER mind was racing after being on-line with Wyllow. 'Of course!' She had shouted when she worked it out. 'It's obvious.' But how had he known the meaning of the code? She wandered up the narrow stairway to finish the job of clearing the loft she had begun earlier. She found a box of papers dating back to her time at Art College, and tipped out the notes from an old loose-leaf folder. She had almost forgotten about her thesis on Renaissance art. There was an illustration lying in front of her under a pool of dim light...

'The Primavera, Botticelli - The painting represents the Paradise garden and forbidden fruit. The name Eve means *first life* or *Spring*....'

Her thoughts turned back to sermon and then to the Italian meal. Her mobile made a beep. She picked it up, but the battery was dead.

****

Adrian yawned, 'I've been at it non-stop all weekend.'

'It's only ten, so, what have we got?' Chris enquired, eagerly.

Adrian pointed at the screen and for several minutes, the scientists chatted excitedly over the results. 'We've been looking for years for something like this. We need to keep the crystal longer.' Adrian stated.

Chris looked at Adrian with a concerned expression. 'There's an email from Stalker, Head of Research – it's a company directive. Everyone has to concentrate all research worldwide on gas fusion polymers.'

'That's crazy!' Adrian was alarmed. 'Haven't you told Stalker exactly how close we are? We're nearly there with molecular memory using the crystal photon laser. At last, quantum mechanics is starting to provide the payback.'

'Stalker's always been against crystals. I didn't want to present the results until we had it cracked, otherwise Stalker would just find fault.' Chris hesitated. 'We're going to release the data when we're ready, and not before.'

'Ok, I'm with you, Chris.' Adrian finished copying the data.

'I'll take the results back with me to Carolina in person.' Chris took the disk from Adrian. 'We can't trust email. Come on,' Chris gestured toward the exit, 'I'll buy you a beer, you've earned one.'

They left the building and walked to Adrian's Citroën. A few minutes later, they entered the pub car park. Chris glanced round at an old Morris that pulled in after them.

They made their way through a sea of people across the noisy lounge and Chris ordered the drinks. He caught a glimpse of a shock of blond hair in the mirror behind the bar. He turned around to see a fleeting figure disappeared through the door.

'Strange…' he said to Adrian, 'that looked just like someone I met down in Dorset.' They took their drinks over to the corner and sat down to plan the next series of tests.

'Here's something that might amuse you.' Adrian took a book out from his small canvas bag and handed it to Chris.

Chris raised his eyebrows at the title 'String Theory and the number Seven'. The painting of the Primavera was on the cover. He opened it and read out loud - 'Doh, Dominus the absolute; Re, Regina coelum the Moon; Mi, the microcosmos the Earth; Fa, fata the planets; Sol the sun; La, lactea the Milky Way; Ti the sidera, all the stars in the sky…'

'And that brings us back to Doh…' Adrian chuckled.

That night in the hotel bedroom, before Chris fell asleep, his thoughts turned to the seven stars of the Pleiades. The stars transformed into maidens performing a ballet. They danced around a hilltop fire. They danced in the shadow of the Cernstone. The leading lady was a figure dressed in white. Her face was like an angel's face. Her face was like Botticelli's Spring. That night, for the first time, her face became clear to Chris - reflected in the firelight was the face of Erica.

CHAPTER 26

The Fence

EVERY NIGHT DURING THAT week, Erica lay awake with her thoughts. Should she admit to Chris how much she missed him? Did he feel the same way? The image of seeing Beth and Chris together kept playing on her mind.

As each day passed, she discovered time was no friend. Far from thinking about Chris less, she found he was on her mind even more.

On Monday, Chris had phoned briefly from the airport. She had asked about the crystal, but frustratingly, he had been cut off. Erica felt she was losing both Chris and the crystal.

On Tuesday, she received a two-word text message… it said 'missing you.' She replied in similar vein. If she were waiting for an explanation of his lunch date with Beth, none came.

On Wednesday, Erica received an email to say that he was in his laboratory in Raleigh, North Carolina. He hoped to let her know about the crystal and that he'd be back in England soon.

On Thursday, she sent him an email in return.

On Friday, Erica took Sarah's brooch to the museum in Dorchester. The official asked her to fill out a form with her phone number and asked her to leave the brooch for a visiting expert from the British Museum to assess the following week. She had lunch in the Paradiso. It brought back more memories of their dinner date. It felt like a month had passed but it had been less than a week.

Erica passed the time shopping until it was time to pick up her husband from the station. She was expecting him to still be livid about the newspaper headlines, from the previous Monday. However, that now seemed like water under the bridge as she could tell from his expression that something else was now occupying his thoughts. She looked at him, warily. He seemed pleased with himself over something.

'I thought I might be able to help Rodney out raising funds for the church.'

'What did you have in mind?' Erica eyed him with distrust. Since when had Simon cared two hoots about the church's finances? Something was afoot, but Simon was unusually reticent.

'Just an idea… might do me a bit of good, locally, can't say any more.' he added. 'I'm off to see him tomorrow with a proposition.'

On Sunday morning, Simon came to the breakfast table eagerly clutching a copy of the colour supplement. 'Guess what?' he exclaimed.

In a combative mood, Erica could not resist a dig. 'You're in a cowpat in glorious Technicolor?'

'Very funny… no, there's an article on your Chris Credus.' Simon read out the headline in a sardonic tone. *'IS THIS THE NEXT BILL GATES?'* He chuckled. 'Personally, I would have thought your Credus was well past it - it makes him out to be some sort of megastar.'

Erica was used to Simon trying to play on her vulnerability. She pretended not to be interested.

Having failed to goad a reaction out of Erica, Simon went off to have a shave.

As soon as he was out the room, Erica grabbed the paper. It was a good photograph. He was sitting casually, in the lounge of the Green Man, with a pint of beer on the table. She stared at it. She could not stop herself. She was mesmerised and wanted to remember every minor detail. She studied the image - his nose, every wrinkle around his deep blue eyes, and his dark brown hair with the patches of grey on each of his temples. She remembered his lace-up brown leather shoes, his blue shirt with small checks, the fine blonde hairs on his tanned forearm against his leather watchstrap and gold buckle, the elegant Roman numerals on the watch.

The gushing terms Beth employed in the piece unsettled her, but at least now she realized why Chris and Beth had been together at lunch the previous Sunday. The article made her want to see him again all the more,

After she had taken her husband to the London train, she breathed a sigh of relief and wondered just what it was that she and Simon still really shared in common - another weekend was over, not a moment too soon.

By early evening, she had read every word of the article in the colour supplement several times over.

Vicky phoned. 'Listen, I've some news for you.' Vicky was agitated. 'You didn't come to the service today but Rodney announced that they're fencing off an area of the Oakenland.'

'What?' Erica was alarmed.

'It's something to do with investigating the ground structure,' explained Vicky. 'There's going to be a public meeting at the Village Hall, on Thursday at eight.'

Later that evening, they sat down in Erica's sunroom with a tray of coffee and biscuits.

'If you have any troubles,' Vicky asked, sympathetically, 'you can tell me.' Vicky had caught an air of abstraction about Erica.

Erica thought for a moment before she let go. 'We don't communicate with each other any more. It's like we are living out the lines of a play. It feels like we are staying together only because we can't afford the risk of doing anything about it. It's better for his political career to be married, and that seems the only reason why we're still together.'

'But at least, you are still together,' Vicky said.

'Only just.' Erica shrugged. 'I'm not sure for how much longer. Simon and I have changed. I can feel it. We have each moved on, each in our own way, and we're still moving apart.'

They stared out through the sunroom window to the garden in the evening light - a robin was diligently carrying nesting material back and forth.

'People do change over time. It doesn't have to be anyone's fault,' reflected Vicky. 'Would Chris Credus have anything to do with this?'

Erica nodded and sipped her coffee and continued. 'Sometimes people even go back in time and find something new buried deep within. I feel empty and hollow inside,' Erica continued. 'It must have been hard bringing up Will on your own, but you have your lovely memories of Rowan. Perhaps you can start again?'

'It's true,' Vicky had an optimistic note in her voice, 'I don't want to be on my own for ever.'

The robin collected twigs and pieces of grass as they talked.

'What's all this about the Oakenland, Vicky? It sounds worrying.'

'Rodney announced at the service this morning, they're fencing part of it off, to carry out geological tests,' Vicky explained, 'looks like they might want to build on the land.'

'But that's terrible.' Erica was horrified.

'The land belongs to the Church and they can do what they want. I'm as upset as you. Rodney said that the church needs funds. He put it across as a good news story and implied this was his last hope. I've tried to argue the point but he says the future of St Michael's is at stake.'

'It doesn't sound like a good news story to me.' Erica said, crossly. 'We'll need to try and find out what's happening.'

'There's to be a question and answer session in the Village Hall on Thursday evening, before the Ladies' Circle meets. I've the feeling it might be to do with those two city types we saw in the tea room.'

'We'll go and ask Rodney, in person,' announced Erica.

'Will has borrowed my car for the weekend,' explained Vicky, 'and I need to go into Witchbury tomorrow for lunch with Sam.'

Erica perked up. 'I'll give you a lift in the morning. We can go to the Manse on the way.'

CHAPTER 27

The Daydream

MONDAY MORNING, THEY DROVE passed the church on the way to the Manse. 'I don't believe it!' Erica pointed at a blue arrow tied to a lamppost and slowed down. 'It looks like work has already started.'

They turned off the road along the gravel track toward the Portal Stone. Fifty yards on, Erica jammed on her brakes. A steel fence topped with barbed wire and a high gate blocked their way, behind which was a mechanical digger. A diminutive figure in a black boiler suit swaggered up to the car. He wore a cap, with a distinctive blue circle around the letters NC. A huge Doberman strained at the lead.

'It's Kneebone…' exclaimed Vicky. 'What's he doing here?'

A husky voice barked at them. 'No admittance, what do you want?'

Vicky looked taken aback 'Since when?' She demanded. 'You don't own this land, Dodo.'

'I'm just carrying out orders. It's my job to keep people out,' Kneebone sneered.

The Doberman let out a ferocious snarl and Jet jumped over between Vicky and Erica and barked, fiercely. In the confines of the car, it put an end to further conversation. In the midst of the din, they had no option but to retreat.

'What shall we do now?' asked Vicky.

Erica was fired-up. 'Go and see Radpole, of course.' 'What's Kneebone doing there?' she demanded.

'That's typical of Dodo. He's officious, and just wants in on everything,' commented Vicky.

They approached the door of the Manse. Erica tugged on the brass pull. In the depths of the house, the bell gave a distant ring.

After what seemed an age, the door opened. Miss Tweedy stood in her grey pinafore. She seemed annoyed at being diverted from her duties.

'We'd like to see Rodney,' Vicky demanded.

'He's gone up to London on important business,' Miss Tweedy replied.

'When he returns, could you please tell him we'd like to see him?' Erica remained as courteous as possible.

'What's it to do with, may I ask?'

'I think he'll know,' replied Vicky.

Miss Tweedy was dismissive. 'He's very busy, you know… He won't be back till late. He's gone to witness a legal document. It'll be tomorrow, now.'

They headed back to the car.

'I'm having lunch with Sam, perhaps he knows something.' Vicky suggested.

'I'll take Jet for a walk on the Hill and pick you up again at two o'clock from the Emporium.' Erica dropped Vicky off, and parked next to the grocery store. The church clock struck noon in the distance. Miss Bird always knew the latest gossip. A queue of people had built up. The grocer seemed to be having problems with a new cash register. Eventually, Erica reached the counter. 'I see you're busy today, Miss Bird.'

'It's this till.' Miss Bird prodded the cash register. 'I hate all this new machinery.'

'Talking about new machinery Miss Bird, do you know what's happening with the Oakenland?'

'It's up to the Church, it's their land,' she said, curtly. 'Better them, than some folks…' she threw a sideways glance towards the grocery shelves.

Who did she mean, 'some folks'? Erica looked around. In the next aisle bobbed a mop of blond hair. By the time she had sorted the money for the bread, there was no one to be seen. Erica wondered if anyone else in the village even cared about the Oakenland. She needed to work out a course of action.

There was still blue sky, but clouds were now gathering out to the west. She would have time to climb to the top of the Hill and be back to pick up Vicky. She returned along the valley road and parked the car in the clearing at the edge of the Oakenland.

As soon as Jet was let out, he bounded off ahead of her. This time she was determined not to let him out of her sight. She climbed steadily, keeping pace with the dog as he hurtled ahead through the woodland and up toward the open heath on the top of the Hill.

Her mind filled with a giddy mixture of images, emotions and nagging doubts. Like pieces of a puzzle, jumbled in a box, one by one, she inspected each piece, and tried to separate them into groups - her marriage, Chris and Beth, Vicky, the crystal and now the threat to the Oakenland - how could she make sense of it all?

When would she be seeing Chris again? He had talked about returning in three weeks, but things seemed to be happening far too quickly. The image of Chris with Beth, in her car after their Sunday pub lunch together, kept replaying in her mind. Was she wrong about him? Despite his words, perhaps he cared more about the crystal than about her.

As she climbed, the distant views through the trees echoed glimpses back through time. The higher she went, the clearer she could see. She reached the top of the Hill, and the freshness of the Spring air revived her spirits. A cool breeze distilled her thoughts. She approached the summit and the landscape began to unfold below her. She looked around at the beauty of the heath. The compulsion grew. She had to act.

A few yards from the Hell Stone, the rocks jutted out like a diving board projecting over the Cauldron below. From the limestone precipice, she peered down the sheer cliff of Devil's Drop. At the bottom, rested the Portal Stone, and a few hundred yards further on was the church. A sudden shiver went through her as she realized how easy it would be to fall.

She looked across the valley. In the far distance, she could make out the sea. The countryside below - a riddle of a place; a place to become lost within, yet where one could find oneself; a place that was like no other on earth.

'You're right…'

The voice behind startled her. She was close to the edge of the cliff. She felt her stomach jump. She stepped back from the precipice and fell into the cushion of someone's arms.

'This place is like no other on earth.' The voice echoed her thoughts exactly.

She turned round. 'You made me jump.'

'I didn't mean to startle you. Hello again, I'm Will.'

Erica was off guard. How did he know what she was thinking? He wore a hand-made jacket. It was a loosely woven faded dark blue wool. Although he was fair, he had a ruddy, outdoor complexion. For a moment, she found herself tongue-tied. She had met him before. Erica stared into his intense, pale blue eyes. 'But, you're Wyllow…'

Jet went up to him, and wagged his tail. Will petted him as if they were old friends.

He nodded. 'I heard you talking, in the shop. This land belongs to us, not the Church. They had no right to take it. The Oakenland and the Hill is our life force. Listen to it. Feel it around you.'

Erica looked about at the open landscape. 'It's beautiful…'

Will guided her away from the precipice and motioned her to sit on the grass. 'This is our land.' He turned and looked directly into her eyes as he spoke. 'Some people in the village don't like us, they think we're just New-Agers.

'How do you know so much about me?'

'Mr Janus bought the computer from me. I set up your system, because I had a feeling you might be sympathetic to our cause.'

'I didn't know you knew Simon.'

'Everyone knows who he is. Jerry in the pub asked if I could set it up for him - I just personalised it a bit. What you said in the shop... you're right to question what's happening.'

'I see...' Erica slowly began to realise what Will had done. She listened to his softly spoken words as he told her of the Celtic tribe and the priestess, and time before recorded history.

'Three thousand years ago, the Hendas lived here, on this very Hill. The Oakenland was their lifeblood. Today we live on, in their spirit. We live as they lived, we uphold their beliefs, and keep the memory alive. We watch and guard the Oakenland and keep it from harm. We follow the ways of the forestfolk, with plants and herbs. We foster prayer, meditation and trance. Through the power of nature, we keep alive their spirit. The Cernstone, the Altar, the Portal - the gateway to the land of our forebears.'

'The Cernstone? You called it that before.' Erica remembered the message on-line.

'The Church calls it the Hell Stone. We call things by their real names and keep stewardship of the Oakenland. We live as a peaceful community. There's no divide between the sacred and the secular. The spirit of the ancients surround us.'

'I understand.' Erica felt she identified with his words. 'Sometimes those values must be difficult to keep.'

Will continued with a far away look in his eyes. 'This is where my father passed into the Otherworld. I want to keep his spirit alive. When I'm here, I'm with him. My father knew them - the Hendas. They're here in the landscape. He told me about them. He communicated with them. His spirit lives through them.'

Erica watched him silently.

Will brushed back strands of long blond hair from off his brow. 'I have something for you.'

She looked down to see a familiar leather thong. 'My ammonite, I thought I'd lost it forever.'

'You left it with us.' Will looked at her puzzled expression and he continued. 'You fell into a trance and Jet led you home. Jet came to us for two nights. The dog was guided by his own spirit and chose to stay. He was free to come back to you, at any time.'

'Will, I understand how you must feel but you know that was wrong...' Erica began. She was alarmed. 'Why didn't you return him?'

Will ignored her pleas. 'Mrs Janus, there's something you don't know; you're daughter was with me.'

'Sarah?' Her mind jumped back to May Eve, when the coats cupboard was in disarray. 'But Sarah was at her friend's...' Erica thought for a second. 'So who left me the gift?'

'It was from the Hendasfolk.' Will let her reach her own conclusion, and continued, 'The Church believes the Oakenland is their land, but they took it from the ancients. Erica, we must protect it. Help us.'

'What can I do?'

'Work with us. The power of the crystal can protect the land.'

Erica looked puzzled. 'The power of the crystal, how? I don't have it, it's in Cambridge.'

'Seek guidance through the spirits, harmonise with the souls of the Hendas, and listen to their voices. We'll call them through their prayer. Close your eyes.'

They sat cross-legged and Will slowly chanted a prayer.

'Kindle our souls from the spark of the stars

Flame of light, flame of love, and flame of life

Kindle our souls from the light of Maia's glory

Truth in our hearts, strength in our hands, vision in our eyes and purpose in our minds

May the power of light and love the power of truth, and vision, energise our souls and guide us to the answer.'

Will made a deep humming sound and Erica found herself instinctively brought into resonance.

At first, all she could hear were the sounds of their own voices, but after a while, the hum drowned out the real world and gathered an energy of its own.

Now, she heard other voices speaking, and saw the scene in her mind. She was looking out over the cliff top towards an arc of light. A tribe gathered around two great fires. A beautiful fair-haired priestess spoke to her softly... 'The gift from the gods... keep it safe.'

CHAPTER 28

The Confrontation

THE FAMILIAR DISTANT CHIME of the church clock struck three. Then, the more persistent sound of the twenty-first century intruded into her half-sleep… Erica's mobile phone was ringing. She opened her eyes. Slowly, she pieced fragments together. The last thing she could recollect was the soft sound of Will's voice - a prayer. How had she managed to get back to her car? The mobile continued to ring. How could she lose an hour? She sat a few seconds more trying to collect her thoughts. What was happening to her? Was she losing her mind? She glanced in the rear view mirror. Jet was fast asleep on the back seat. She put her hand to her neck and she was comforted to feel the leather thong. 'Damn, I was meant to pick up Vicky at two o'clock.' Erica was alarmed. She took her phone from the glove compartment. It was Vicky.

'What happened to you? Sam gave me a lift instead. Are you OK? I tried your mobile, but there was no answer. I thought, perhaps you had dropped off to sleep?"

'The battery keeps playing up. I'm really sorry for letting you down.' Erica hesitated. 'I seem to have lost an hour somewhere.' She felt unable to tell Vicky what had really happened. She was not even sure herself. 'Vicky, perhaps we can meet up tonight when I'm more together? I'll come over to your place.' Erica put away the phone, and stared up to the top of the cliff and the Hell Stone. Will had called it the Cernstone and an image of Cernunnos from the Gundestrup Cauldron came into her mind.

When Erica arrived home, Sarah wearing a hippy-style gypsy dress met her. 'Do you know where the brooch is mum?'

'I took it to Dorchester for a valuation. We might need to insure it. Where are you off to?'

'Out,' her daughter replied in a frustrated tone. 'Don't wait up.' Sarah looked preoccupied. 'I'll eat out with my friends.'

'Look after yourself wherever you're going… and take your mobile. I'm off to Vicky's tonight.' Erica watched through the window as her daughter headed off in the direction of the Hill. Now she knew her daughter was involved with Will, she would have to find the right time to discuss with her.

The phone rang. It was Sam. 'I have some news for you…' he began, 'the test results on the sample of bath oil you gave me.'

****

Vicky already had a pot of coffee waiting when Erica arrived at the Four Winds. They sat in the kitchen and watched the clouds cover the dusky sky.

'I totally misjudged Chris.' Erica shook her head. 'Let's face it; he's not interested in me, he's only interested in his bloody research.'

Vicky was feeling Erica's turmoil. 'So, you've not heard from him?'

Erica shook her head. 'Not much…'

Vicky tried to console her. 'Perhaps you could write to Chris and just let him know what you're feeling? Or you could try phoning him?'

'I don't know what I want.' Erica was distraught.

Vicky reached out and touched her hand for a few seconds. 'I understand how you feel, but will it help to get so upset?'

Erica sat up straight in the chair and composed herself. 'You're right.' She changed the tone of her voice. 'There's something we need to talk about.'

'Go on, I'm listening.' Vicky looked apprehensive.

'This afternoon, after I dropped you off in the village, I went for a walk with Jet on the Hill and I met Will. That's why I was late.'

'Will?' Vicky was surprised.

'I've not told you before...' Erica paused, 'mainly because I wasn't sure about it myself.'

'What haven't you told me?'

'Will and Wyllow are the same person. He takes on a different identity and leads this group.' Erica tried to relate how she had visited the Beltane fires, and met the Hendasfolk.

Vicky sighed. 'I know he's with some sort of re-enactment ancient history group, is that what you mean? They reconstruct the way of life of the Celts.'

Erica continued. 'The birthday gift was sent from them, it was derived from a plant essence.'

'I agree it's unusual for a boy to be into aromatherapy,'

'Vicky, it's more than aromatherapy. I asked Sam to have the remains of the bottle analysed for me. Just before I came out to see you tonight, he phoned me with the results - the analysis came up with extract of Liberty Cap mushrooms.'

Vicky was shocked. 'Sam didn't tell me.' She paused to consider things, then continued. Will has always been fascinated by chemistry and physics, perhaps he sees it as part of that?'

'There's something else.'

Vicky looked anxiously at Erica.

'Will and Sarah seem to be involved - so you can understand my worries. Before this afternoon, I didn't know it was Will who was behind it,' explained Erica,

'Will is headstrong. He's too much for me at times.' Vicky tried to hold back the emotion in her voice. 'I can't think he meant any harm by it. He's a good boy at heart, but he just gets carried away with all sorts of notions. He seems to have let the pagan thing take him over.' Vicky became thoughtful. 'The ancients used plants to reach a heightened state of consciousness. Like his dad, he must be trying to copy them.'

Erica was concerned. 'Perhaps he's taken things too far…'

'What can I do?' Vicky implored. 'If he's out of control, it's because of Rowan,' Vicky confided. 'His dad believed the ancients spoke to him directly and so does Will. He says it's in the landscape.'

'I can understand.' Erica nodded. 'I feel it too, when I'm out there.' She gestured toward the Hill.

'In the end, Rowan believed he was a shaman and it took him over. They found him on the Portal Stone.' Vicky paused before she continued.'

Erica held Vicky's hand.

'The coroner found traces of a hallucinogen, but it was left as an open verdict. Will is so like Rowan in many ways. Like his father, he's obsessive almost autistic. I've tried to talk to him, but it's made him more secretive. He doesn't tell me anything now.'

Erica put her arm around her. 'Will must have felt the loss deeply, but drugs are dangerous, they can affect different people in different ways… and if Sarah's involved…' Erica broke off.

'Don't contact the police will you,' Vicky shook her head in despair. 'I don't think he meant any harm.'

Erica tried to reassure her. 'We need to deal with this ourselves. No doubt he had his reasons.'

'Rowan used to talk about going to another world. I used to think he meant a different mental world, into his trance states,' Vicky sobbed, 'but he meant the journey to the Otherworld. Will sees the Hill and the area around it as the embodiment of the spirit of Rowan. That's why he feels so protective about the Oakenland.' Vicky stopped crying and suddenly became ready to act. 'I'll phone Sam, he'll know what to do.'

****

Chris had arranged to meet the geologist at an out of town truckstop.

Leo greeted Chris as he walked over to his table in the diner. 'You certainly chose the right place. I feel like a pork chop at a Jewish wedding. Why all the secrecy?' Leo grinned, nervously, and glanced around at the redneck truck drivers. They stared back at him.

'Don't worry, it's nothing illegal.' said Chris. 'I just needed somewhere off the beaten track, and this is about halfway, geographically between your base and mine. Did you get the data analysed I sent from the site investigations?'

Leo nodded.

'So what have you come up with?'

'Ejectile beds,' Leo said, without emotion.

Chris looked at him in astonishment and repeated the words. Some rednecks turned their heads and smirked over their root beers.

'The pattern of the data looks that way,' declared the geologist, in a matter of fact tone. 'There's also a layer of carbon deposits from about three thousand years ago.'

Chris paused thoughtfully as the implication sank in. 'You're suggesting we're looking at a meteorite.'

'A small one,' Leo frowned, 'but that's what the data points to. The carbon suggests a forest fire, but the give-away is the iridium.'

They drank their way through several coffees as they discussed the size of the impact crater and likely magnitude of the meteorite.

On the journey back to base, a thought was taking hold. Chris tried to suppress it, but he was unable to think of anything else. He had never allowed personal emotions to affect his work, but previously, he had never experienced feelings as deep as this. For the first time in his life, work had started to take second place. His waking hours had been spent thinking about Erica, and his sleeping hours dreaming about her. By the time he arrived back at the university the thought had become a compulsion - he was not certain of the outcome but he needed to see her. There was only one answer. To tell her face-to-face that he was missing her like crazy. He needed to return the crystal. He had to return to Dorset.

When Chris returned to the lab, an email from Sam was waiting for him. If he had not spent that rainy Saturday with Sam, and then heard Erica speak so passionately about the Oakenland, he might not have understood why anyone would be concerned about a fence.

Sam answered the phone, sleepily. 'Chris, you do know it is 5am here?'

'Sorry Sam, but I had to phone. I got your email, what's all this about someone fencing off the site?' Chris asked.

'There's a meeting in the Village Hall tonight, I'll let you know what I find out. Erica's very concerned about the Oakenland.'

'Sam, I need to see her - I'll tell you all about it when I get back over. I'll try and be down in Dorset on Sunday. Now listen Sam, Erica gave me the clue when we were on the train. You remember... she said it might have fallen out of the sky, so I contacted Leo, my geologist buddy.

That would also explain why there are no other deposits in the area. Ahhh...' Sam became animated. 'Why didn't I think of it? That's why it's perfect - zero gravity.'

'You got it in one, Sam.' Chris continued. 'Crystals in meteors can form by chemical vapour deposition. It's virtually the same process that's used in manufacturing artificial diamonds. If the crystal were inside a geode from space, like a ripe walnut, the shell could still be out there, and I have a hunch where the two halves are. Sam, I'm coming back over.'

CHAPTER 29

The Meeting

WITCHBURY VILLAGE HALL SAT opposite the Green Man at the heart of the community. That evening, it was alive with activity. Erica and Vicky had taken seats behind Sam at the end of a middle row. Erica noted the full complement of the Ladies' Circle occupied the front row and at their centre, Beebee was buzzing. At the rear of the hall, a motley group of teenagers engaged in an excited conspiratorial huddle. In amidst the group, mirroring the activity of her mother, Dee seemed unusually animated.

Erica was disappointed there was no sign of Will. She looked at Vicky and nodded toward the presence of two men on the stage.

Her friend's expression confirmed she too had recognised the two smartly dressed men in grey silk suits, who they had encountered, barely two weeks before, in the Chocolate Tea Pot.

Next to the Reverend behind the trestle table, sat an empty chair.

Rodney Radpole stood up. 'Good evening, ladies and gentlemen.' The hall hushed. Beebee ceased full flow, and sat in rapt attention. 'We won't keep you long. The Circle will be holding their regular Thursday meeting immediately afterwards. However, I can tell from the attendance, this matter is of great interest to all of you.'

The main doors squeaked. Erica and Vicky turned to see Simon arriving with Beth Frank.

The Reverend caught Simon's eye. 'We're privileged tonight to have, the Honourable Simon Janus, Member of Parliament for Wessex South.'

The MP strode to the front, jumped up on the stage, and acknowledged the ripple of applause. Simon took the empty seat.

Erica glared at him. What had her husband been up to? If he was involved with the fence, no wonder he had tried to keep his activity secret from her.

Radpole continued. 'I think you all know the purpose of this evening, however for everyone's benefit, I'll explain. This meeting has been arranged to inform you of the plans for the site. It's with great pleasure I can make public some very interesting news.' Radpole turned to look at the one of the men in suits. 'Mr Schneider has kindly agreed to come along tonight to represent New Construct, the company who will be carrying out ground trials for foundations.' Radpole nodded with a look of self-satisfaction towards the man with the gold tooth. 'The funds promised will enable St Michael's to continue for some time to come. Over the next few weeks, provided consent is given, NC have offered a very generous donation to St Michael's roof fund.'

The front row clapped. Bunty Bagwash wore an oversized black and gold rugby shirt. Her hand shot up.

Radpole smiled at her, genially. 'Beebee?'

She glowed back at the Reverend. 'I'm sure I speak for all of us here in congratulating you, Rodney, in so expertly negotiating to ensure the church receives adequate recompense.'

Erica cringed.

Radpole was effusive. 'Your words of support are most appreciated.' The Reverend gestured to Miss Tweedy seated at the end of that row, waving her hand. 'Yes, Edith?'

She stood and addressed the meeting in her prim Scottish brogue. 'I'd just like everyone to understand how much this means to us, and how thankful we are that we can continue to live at the Manse.'

Schneider gave a wave of acknowledgement. 'We will do our best to make sure of that, my good lady.' His gold tooth gleamed.

'Perhaps I might also add,' Simon had an up-beat note in his voice, 'Witchbury Cricket Club will also become the proud owners of a new pavilion.'

There was further round of applause from the front row.

Erica seethed.

Radpole continued. 'Without more ado, I have pleasure in asking Mr Schneider… to present the proposals.'

The man with the gold tooth stood up to a ripple of applause. He addressed the audience in clipped tones. 'The preliminary work will take a few months. For reasons of Health and Safety, it's necessary the investigations are fenced off.' He pointed at a map. 'The first phase involves the vicinity of Cauldron Field. We need to establish the exact location of any underground voids from old mine workings.'

In front of her, Sam held up his hand.

Radpole caught his eye. 'Professor?'

'Surely Planning Consent is required?'

Simon stood up. 'Perhaps I can answer… As some of you may have noticed, Phase One fencing work has already begun. This is of a temporary nature so permission is not required. Some of the procedure may involve small explosive charges but it shouldn't be disruptive in any way.'

At the mention of explosive charges, Radpole looked uneasy.

Miss Bird, who was sitting on her own against the side aisle, became agitated. 'No-one said nothing about no explosions. It'll scare my chickens, so it will. They won't lay if they gets upset.'

'Miss Bird,' Radpole turned across the podium. 'Perhaps I could ask Mr Schneider to allay your fears.'

'Should your chickens be in any way put off by our operations, please be assured Miss Bird, you'll receive adequate compensation.' Straight-faced, the businessman sat back and added, 'Could I introduce someone most of you will already know, Mr Dodo Kneebone has agreed to be our community liaison officer.'

Kneebone clambered up onto the stage. His appearance was greeted with a mixture of catcalls and wolf whistles from the teenagers at the back of the hall.

The Reverend looked briefly toward the heavens and grimaced. 'I'm sure everybody finds it reassuring that there are such close ties with the village.' Dodo proudly removed his NC baseball hat, took a bow.

Radpole continued, 'Now, I'll ask our Member of Parliament, Simon Janus, to say a few more words.'

Simon stood up and once more addressed the meeting. 'This is good news for Witchbury. Assuming that the formality of permission is granted for Phase Two, it will bring in much needed funds to the village and it will lead to prosperity in the future... once the affordable housing development is underway.'

'I don't believe it!' The passion of Erica's voice stopped Simon in full flow. She had been sitting with an increasing sense of outrage and could no longer hold back. She rose to her feet and began to march up the aisle toward the stage. She repeated her exclamation.

Murmurs swelled around the room.

The Reverend tried to give counsel. 'Mrs Janus, if you could just return to your seat.'

Erica stalked up to the foot of the podium and spoke stiffly. 'I would like to ask my husband a question. How much will the houses sell for?' Erica fumed.

Everyone waited for Simon to respond.

Simon shuffled sheepishly from side to side. 'As you know, the local area is in desperate need of housing.' He hesitated. 'It's too early to say exactly how much. With the favourable market maybe a mill...'

The hall rocked with an ear-splitting explosion.

Half the audience dropped to the floor. Thick white smoke billowed off the stage and enveloped the auditorium. An acrid smell permeated the air. A moment later, the lights flickered and went out. Chaos struck.

Beebee let out an ear-piercing scream, 'Terrorists!' Like an icebreaker, she cut through the sea of chairs. Empty seats toppled in her wake. Erica watched the shadows on the stage flee for the exit.

A minute later, Erica along with most of the occupants of the hall had escaped the turmoil and stood in the car park, coughing and spluttering. White smoke poured from the main door, and dispersed high up into the air.

Erica and Vicky had separated and Erica glanced up and down Silver Street looking for her. Two figures were running away. 'Sarah and Will, what are they doing?'

Kneebone appeared. 'Pay attention... pay attention everyone.' Dodo climbed precariously onto a high wall and stood above the heads of his audience. He shouted out a pronouncement in an officious, nasal twang. 'Owing to unforeseen circumstances, we are unable to continue the meeting. Move away everybody...' He tottered on the top of the wall. 'The Village Hall is a no-go area until the bomb squad get here.'

'What about our Circle...' Beebee demanded, indignantly.

Kneebone jumped down. 'Make way, make way.' He tried to clear a path through the crowd for a silver BMW.

Ensconced within were Simon, the property developers, and the Reverend. Erica stared in disbelief as the car sped off.

From behind there were a series of bursts from a flash gun. She turned. It was Beth with a camera. Slowly, things became clear - the meeting had not been brought to a halt by a terrorist attack, but by a smoke bomb.

Beth came up to Erica. 'Well... that went off with a bang. I'd be interested in your angle on all this Mrs Janus.' The journalist asked.

Erica was wary but she was feeling livid with Simon.

Beth continued. 'I got the impression you were a little in the dark about your husband's plans. I don't know about you, but I could murder a G&T.' Beth nodded over toward the Green Man. 'Shall we go over to the snug?'

Erica shrugged. What did she have to lose? They headed toward the bar.

CHAPTER 30

The Revelation

SAM PICKED UP THE receiver. He was unaccustomed to phone calls before breakfast, especially on Sunday morning. It was Chris. From the tone in his voice, Sam knew something was wrong. 'Where are you?'

'At Stansted airport. I've got news. The crystal's missing.'

'How did that happen?'

'Last night - a break-in at the Cambridge lab. They knew what they were after. Adrian discovered it first thing this morning. He's driving me down. We should be there in about four hours. I have a hunch that it was someone we know. I need to see Erica.'

'She phoned me last night,' said Sam. 'She's making some sort of announcement, at the Portal Stone at noon.'

'We'll be there.' Chris sounded determined.

****

A padlocked security gate barred access to the Portal Stone. Gathered in front, stood Erica, Vicky, and Sam.

The church clock struck twelve and three more figures came along the path to join them.

'Thank you all for coming.' She also nodded a greeting toward the journalist with a camera who was with Will and Sarah. 'I've invited Beth here to record events. Sam tells me we are expecting two more but, in the meantime, we'll begin. Erica nodded to Will.

He reached into his canvas holdall and held up a pair of bolt cutters. Erica was quick to grab one of the handles and together they sliced through the security chain. Keen to photograph the action, Beth got in close.

The gates swung open and they moved through and gathered around the Portal Stone. Erica jumped up on the Stone and turned to the group. 'I want to make something plain. Some of you may have already seen this - I have no regrets.' She waved a copy of the Sunday paper. They could see the headlines - *Exclusive - MP in Furore over Church Land Deal...*'

Vicky looked perturbed.

'I didn't realise Simon was involved,' Erica continued, 'not until the public meeting on Thursday. When I found out, I was furious. Beth asked me to comment and what you see before you, is the result.'

Erica stood resolute on the Portal. 'The Oakenland belongs to everyone, it's our heritage.' Helped by Beth, they spread out the Sunday broadsheet upon the Portal. 'Simon and I have had our differences in the past but this is the end. I'll ask Beth to read the article.'

Beth too jumped up on top of the Portal. 'MP Simon Janus was criticised yesterday, for being at the centre of an attempt to sell off a Dorset heritage site. New Construct, a development company with international backing are intent on pursuing planning permission for luxury housing. The matter has caused a split between the MP and his wife. When asked to comment, Mrs Janus stated, 'The site is of supreme ecological, cultural and historical importance and should be left undisturbed for the locals to enjoy.'

Will looked at Sarah and nodded. They moved in closer. Sarah spoke up. 'We have a confession to make. It was us that let off the smoke bomb in the Village Hall. It was the only way we knew.'

'It's all right Sarah,' Erica glanced across at Vicky, 'we're all on the same side here.'

Vicky looked apprehensive. 'Does Rodney know?'

A scatter of gravel disturbed them. They turned to see from behind a bush the shadow of Kneebone running off in the direction of the Manse.

'If the Reverend hasn't already read the paper,' Beth said, dryly, 'he's about to find out.'

They heard the crunch of wheels. A few moments later, Chris and Adrian ran through the gate toward them.

Erica jumped down from the stone and raced to Chris. He greeted her with a hug.

Everyone gathered in a circle around the Portal. Will and Sarah took a step forward. Will looked remorseful as his stare flitted from face to face. 'We have another confession,' he said and glanced across to Chris and Erica. From the canvas bag, Will held up something in the air. 'We had to bring it back to its rightful place.'

'The crystal!' Erica gasped.

Sam cut in. 'Will, to take what did not belong to you was wrong.'

'I'm sorry uncle, but I didn't know how else to act.' Will tried to explain. 'Can't you see, the Oakenland, and the Icera Stone, they belong to us all!'

Sam turned to Chris. 'What do you think Dr Credus?'

'I will tell you what we have found out about your Icera Stone. Three thousand years ago,' Chris began, 'a meteorite fell from space. It struck the earth about where we now are standing. It formed a crater and the Cauldron Field was the result. The geode broke in two, as alike as two halves of the shell. The Portal, what we see before us, is one half of that shell. The other half the Celts moved to the top of the Hill, believing it to be a gift from their gods. '

Will held the crystal above the Portal. 'Rowan told me once, how he had seen a vision - a star from the heavens.' Will placed the crystal in the hollow at the centre of the Portal. 'My father knew intuitively the secret of the firestar and what it contained - the gift from the gods - the Icera Stone'

They all stared at the crystal. Blue reflections glinted over their faces.

The Tenor Bell began to toll.

****

That evening, in the light from the log fire in the lounge of the Green Man, an open bottle of champagne stood on ice. Chris and Erica sat on the leather sofa. She breathed a sigh of relief. 'Thank goodness we escaped.'

Chris poured them both a drink and held her hand.

She looked at him with affection. 'Simon's gone to ground. I don't blame him, with the press corps camped out behind our front hedge, but it was the only way to stop the Oakenland being carved up for profit. I knew he would never listen to me.'

'I have some news...' Chris paused. He watched Erica's expression change to curiosity. He took out an object from his pocket. 'Hold out your hand.' Something small touched her palm. Instinctively, she brought it to her breast. Twenty-five years ago, the ammonite had been broken. Now again, the two halves interlocked once more to form the perfect spiral. Pieces that for years had been apart now were back as one. 'I'm coming back to England, I want us to be together.'

'Chris, how wonderful, I knew it must be you. I'm so happy.'

****

Some weeks later, a vintage BSA motorbike leant against the apple tree outside Four Winds.

Vicky stood by the window as she looked at a cheque made out from the British Museum. 'In the end, your prayers were answered, Rodney; St Michael's lives on.'

The Reverend walked over to her. 'The donation will secure the future, for a few more years. At least we can stay at the Manse, and I won't be going to Birmingham.' He smiled. 'I suppose there is a certain irony in the church being saved by Pagans.'

'You have Sarah and Will to thank for donating the proceeds of the Beltane Brooch,' Vicky returned his smile. 'It was a rare find.'

'So are you, Vicky.' The Reverend took her hand. 'Come and sit down here next to me on the sofa. Vicky, I've something to ask you, and I'm hoping you're going to say, yes.'

THE EPILOGUE

Ten Years Later

AT NUMBER 10, A thirty-three year old researcher in a black dress, diamante necklace and ringlets of burnished copper brought coffee into the Cabinet Room. From the head of the conference table, Simon Janus threw her a familiar glance.

****

In Stockholm, in the audience of the auditorium of the concert hall, Chris held Erica's hand. She smiled and tightened her grip.

At the microphone, the announcer from the Swedish Institute of Sciences proclaimed, 'For the development of the Quantum Computer based on entangled photons, the Nobel prize for Physics is awarded to - Will Fellows.'

Will stepped up onto the podium, his long blond locks at odds with his stiff white collar. 'I would like to thank the following for their guidance and inspiration,' he looked earnestly at the audience. 'My mother Vicky, my late father Rowan and, back in Witchbury, my great uncle Sam, who proved to me how close science is to magic. I would also like to thank four other people, without whom this would not have been possible - my assistant Adrian, Dr Christopher Credus, his wife the celebrated artist Erica Credus, and of course her daughter, my wife, Sarah.'

'Finally, yet importantly, I would also like to pay my respects to the Hendas. It is their legacy that has enabled us to take the next step on our ladder to the stars.'

The audience burst into enthusiastic applause.

Will smiled, reached into his pocket, 'Ladies and Gentlemen...' He held up the crystal, it sparkled under the spotlights. 'The Icera Stone.'

****

On his bed in Witchbury, an old man lay content, surrounded by memories. He stared at the Botticelli on the wall. His eyes rested upon the beauty of the lady in white. She seemed to beckon to him. He allowed himself to be drawn through into another world where the brightest star shone.

In Dorchester, Sarah, gave birth to a daughter, Seren. In the sky above, a distant star slowly faded and a new one was born.

ABOUT THE AUTHOR:

Andrew Homer

Andrew graduated with a First Class Honours in Architecture from the University of Newcastle upon Tyne.

Andrew has a life-long interest in art, mythology and science. He now lives in Cornwall.

The Icera Stone is his first novel.

Printed in the United Kingdom
by Lightning Source UK Ltd.
127434UK00002B/172-189/A